Other books by the author:

On The Boulevard
Purple Adobe
Whose Name I Did Not Know
Claw Hammer

SNAPSHOT

CHRIS HELVEY

LIVINGSTON PRESS

THE UNIVERSITY OF WEST ALABAMA

ISBN 13: 978-1-60489-197-3, hardcover
ISBN 13: 978-1-60489-196-6 trade paper
ISBN: 1-60489-197-1 hardcover
ISBN: 1-60489-196-3 trade paper
Library of Congress Control Number 2017948799
Printed on acid-free paper
by Publishers Graphics
Printed in the United States of America

Hardcover binding by: Heckman Bindery
Typesetting and page layout: Sara Coffey and Joe Taylor
Proofreading: Joe Taylor, Sara Coffey, Shelby Parrish
Cover design: Té Duffour and Amanda Nolin

Cover photo: Amanda Nolin
Author photo: Clay Gibson

This is a work of fiction:
any resemblance
to persons living or dead is coincidental.

Livingston Press is part of The University of West Alabama,
and thereby has non-profit status.
Donations are tax-deductible:
brothers and sisters, we need 'em.

first edition
6 5 4 3 3 2 1

This novel is for Joe Taylor, whose support, dedication, an editorial guidance were instrumental in making it a reality.

SNAPSHOT

1

THE WHOLE SKY WAS spider-webbed with red and gold when we drug our tired bodies out of the mouth of Black John Mine No. 3. At least all the sky a man could see. On the morning side of that mountain it was already going dark. Off to the west, the sun was sliding down the curve of the earth. A line of clouds hung low on the horizon, and when the sun dropped behind them they went as purple as wild grapes.

I walked out that evening with J.D. Purvis and Lonnie Crawford. All week it had been warm for November, but as the sun began to fade the air grew cooler. A light breeze had sprung up since we'd gone in and I shivered and wished for my jacket.

By the time we climbed the little rise and leveled out on Croley Ridge we were walking through the last patch of sunlight and I was starting to sweat under my clothes. The walnut trees had all gone bare, and you could see nuts hanging like Christmas ornaments with the color baked out of them. Gum trees were splashes of red and gold all mixed together and a few of the sugar maples that grew in the shelter of the limestone were still scarlet. The leaves on the big oaks had gone bronze and started to fall and when you walked through them the fallen leaves made a swishing sound that made me remember when I was a kid and my brothers and I would rake leaves for Widow Grogan and old man Thomas and Miss

Martha Vanhoose who gave piano lessons and never had married.

We'd spend all of one Saturday pushing leaves into the biggest pile in Buhlan County. Just afore dusk, my brother Ancil, who was the oldest, would bum a match off Mr. Thomas who was always home on account of his leg which had gotten mangled in the Benham Mine accident back in '37. Once Ancil had the match, all of us boys would gather round and watch him light a dry patch of leaves and blow gentle on the fire until the whole pile caught and you could see flames all the way to Guthrie.

Ancil was gone now. Run over by a coal train when his old Ford stalled on the tracks and he'd fiddled too long with the ignition. Fact was, all my brothers was gone. At least they'd had left out of Buhlan County and I didn't know where any of them were, except for Johnny, who was in the state pen down at Eddyville for killing the youngest Colegrove boy outside a tavern down in Richmond. None of us Burke boys had much of a head for liquor. Some got to wanting to fight and others took on a crying jag. Whiskey or beer, didn't matter much to me. Both got me all worked up for a woman.

At the ridge point, I said good-bye to J.D. and Lonnie. They both turned left and went down the hill toward Sawyers. I took the path, you couldn't call her a road now, that curled around the hill and crossed Mercy Creek and the old Cumberland Turnpike before it finally wore itself out in the head of Griffin Holler. At least that was what most people called it. I had another name for the patch of ground where my family had lived for five generations.

A series of swells buckled the ridge, and in the depressions wild ferns grew and the last of the wildflowers drooped their aging heads. After a bit, I came up a slope steeper than the rest and found myself on Witches Point. At the very end, alone among the rocks, was a huge old hickory. For as long as I could remember it had been dying and on this early November afternoon it looked as dead as a hammer. A red hawk swayed on a narrow limb at the very top. He was facing west. My Grandpa Schlumer would have said that was a sign death was coming.

I'd just started down the slope again when I heard somebody calling my name. Having just seen that hawk and then hearing my name called gave me a start and a shiver traveled my spine. I whirled around and watched Turp Lawson jog down the slope.

"Hey, Eddie. How you doing?"

"Okay, Turp," I said, wondering why he wanted to see me. And, if he had something to say why hadn't he said it back at the mine. For almost two years I'd worked with Turp and we probably hadn't talked more than a half dozen times.

He came alongside and I turned and started walking toward the house. If he wanted to talk then he could walk with me.

We walked on for maybe fifty yards before he started talking again.

"You and some of the guys get together for a little drinking sometimes, don't you?"

"Been known to lift a bottle."

"Well, I like a drink, too, every now and then, you know. I mean it's not like I drink every night. Just once in a while, see?"

"Guess you can drink whenever you're a mind to."

"Sure, only I get a little tired drinking alone, and I

was wondering if maybe I could get together with you guys sometime. I'm gonna get some shine this weekend. What do you think?"

I didn't say anything for a minute. Just didn't know what to say. Turp Lawson wasn't a guy I had much desire to drink with. He was alright, I guess. Only a little soft in a way that made you wonder what he'd be like in a fight.

"Where you gonna get your shine?"

"Soon as I get a payday I'm going over on Leech Branch and get a quart off Speck Miller."

"Thought old Speck was in a bad way. Last I heard he had the stomach cancer."

"Yeah, the old man's real sick. Going to buy it from his boy, Junior."

A squirrel was squawking up in a burr oak and I turned my head until I spied him way out on a limb. I hadn't had fried squirrel in a long time and I wished for my shotgun.

"Don't know that I'd buy anything off Junior Miller. Can't swear this, but Tommy Cox told me that his cousin bought shine off Junior last year and before he got half a pint drunk he was stone blind."

Turp laughed a little then and punched me on the arm, which I didn't much care for. Don't like for any man, or woman, to put their hands on me unless I knew them a hell of a lot better than I knew Turp Lawson.

"Ah, Junior's alright. He's giving me a real deal. Aim to buy all my shine from him."

I didn't say anything, only nodded and kept on slogging along. It had been a long day in a 36-inch seam and I was tired and hungry.

"So, what do you think?"

"Think about what?"

"About me drinking with you and J.D. and Lonnie next Friday."

I shrugged. "I'll ask them," I said.

"Sounds fine," he said and stuck his hand out. Even though I didn't want to, I shook it. He grinned like he'd found a silver dollar in his bean soup.

"Oh, one more thing," Turp said, and drug his boot through the dirt. He hung his head like some shy kid on the schoolyard. Then he peeked up from under a shock of dirty blonde hair. "My wife and I, we was wondering if you wanted to come to dinner Sunday." He lifted his head and smiled and right then he looked so young and eager that I felt sorry for him.

Besides being surprised as hell, the only feeling I had was embarrassment. Wasn't sure whether I was embarrassed for him or for myself. I didn't know what to say. Nobody had ever asked me to come to Sunday dinner. Hate to hurt a man's feelings unless I have to, and in the end I nodded and said, "Okay."

"Good," he said. "We eat early. My wife will be glad to meet you. Been telling her all about you and the other guys at the mine."

"Didn't know you were married."

"Yes." Turp said, "Married Marta Reynolds back in the summer. Fourth of July." He was grinning again.

"Never heard anything about it. Congratulations."

"Thanks." His grin got bigger. "She's a real pretty girl."

I could hear the wind whispering in the pines lower along the ridge. That was a lonesome sound. The sun had gone down now, and a chill threaded through the air. A wave of tiredness washed through me and I wanted to sit down. Instead, I nodded at Turp and said, "Getting dark,

I better be headed home and so had you. That wife of yours will be waiting."

"Yeah," he said and grinned again and I guess right then I hated him a little bit. Hatred's a bad thing in a man. I knew that. Hatred will eat your insides up worse than the cancer. I'd hated enough in my life to know that there was nothing good in it. So I just said "See you," and turned and started walking toward the holler. He said something after me, but I just waved a hand and kept on walking. It was nigh on dark and I was tired and hungry and way too lonely to listen to any more about Turp Lawson's pretty new wife. Halfway up the next slope, I turned and look back. All I could see was an empty path and the air going purple and the oak leaves shivering in the wind.

2

NIGHT WAS FALLING hard by the time I made the head of the holler. Most people called it Griffin Holler, after Clyde Griffin who lived there back in the 30's and served two tours as Sheriff before somebody ambushed him one Easter morning as he was driving home from sunrise services.

Like I said, most people call it Griffin Holler, but I call it Lonesome Holler. Since my dad died back last winter and my wife left me in the spring, that's all that old holler has felt like. Pure blue lonesome.

To tell the truth, there wasn't much left in the old holler, whatever name you called it. Back in the 40's, over seventy-five people lived in there. Better than a dozen families. Even when I was a kid there were still twenty-five or thirty people living there. Number depended on how many of the Ratliff boys was at home and how many was in jail.

Now, there weren't but three of the houses occupied. Mine was at the very top of the holler, just before the timberline. Asa Washington lived in the first house on the left after you turned off the trail. Asa was an old black man, crippled with the arthritis so that he hardly ever left his porch. One of his boys brought him groceries and mail every Saturday. Asa always had a light burning in his house. One time I asked him about that and he said he left a lamp burning all the time because since his eyesight had started to go the shadows cast by the lamp looked like people to him and seeing those shadows flickering on the walls made him fell less lonely.

The lamp in his kitchen was burning tonight and I waved, just in case he was looking, then trudged on up the narrowing path. The next three houses were empty. In fact, one of them, the old Hensley place, had burnt down on New Year's Eve. Kids looking for something to do had taken to squatting in there on the weekends, and I guess they didn't tend good to their fire.

Beyond the chimney that was all that was left of the Hensley place was the house where the Davis sisters lived. They were a couple of old maids, probably in their fifties now and big and strong as most men. Neither Idell nor Lois were much to look at, but they was both nice and once Idell had baked me a pie for Christmas. Butterscotch, my favorite.

After I got past the Davis sisters, there were only broken out window glass and doors swinging open on their hinges and porches with the eaves caving in. Any time of day it was a sad, lonely patch of ground, but it always seemed worst in the twilight. I hurried on, and in a minute I heard the barking of my dog, Trips.

Trips got his name when he was a pup and always stumbling over his own big feet. He wasn't any special kind of dog. Just an ordinary hound. But he was always glad to see me.

Trips got wind of my scent and quit barking and came loping out of the darkness and jumped up and put his paws on me and licked my hands until I scratched behind his ears. Then he trotted along at my side as I turned off the path and went in around the back of the house. Since Karen left I'd gotten in the habit of coming in the kitchen door.

I fumbled around in the near dark, found a match and lit the kerosene lantern on the table. Guess the holler is about the last place left in the county where they haven't run the electric.

There wasn't any wood in the box and I stumbled back out into the gathering darkness and gathered up some from the shed. I was starting to run low. Summers are when I get lazy.

In a few minutes I had a good fire burning and went out in the back yard and pumped a bucket of water from the well my grandfather and his brothers had dug. Some people claim acid is leeching out of the mines and tainting the water, but mine was still cool and clear and tasted good. I poured some in Trips' bowl and gave him a fistful of Old Roy dog food.

Thinking about nothing important, I washed my face and hands. Then I roamed around the kitchen trying to figure out what to eat. It had been close to two weeks since I'd been to town and the pickings were slim. Trips was already licking at his bowl.

In the end, I settled for cold cornbread and the last of the soup beans I'd cooked a couple of days before. While I ate I thought about Turp Lawson asking me to break bread with him and his wife.

Wanting to go drinking with me and J.D. and Lonnie I could understand. But asking me to come over for a meal perplexed me. But what seemed strangest of all was that Turp would get married. Not that there was necessarily anything wrong with Turp. He was just sort of scrawny and had a long thin nose and little piggy eyes set close together. Still, as far as I knew, he did a fair day's work and kept himself clean and most of the time he shaved. He was neither ugly nor good looking. And I guess he wasn't what you would call a mean man. So there was nothing really wrong with him. No, it was more that for some reason I couldn't name that I'd never figured him for the marrying kind.

After supper, I heated water and washed and dried my dishes. Then Trips and I meandered outside. I sat down on the back step and Trips sniffed around at the edge of the light. An owl started hooting over in a grove of hickories. It was old Shorty. I'd named him that because his hoots were always cut short, like someone had chopped the end off of them with a hatchet.

I rolled one while I listened to Shorty, then drew smoke into my lungs. I blew it out and called for Trips. He trotted over and settled down at my feet. After awhile, I could see the evening star and then the moon drifted in among the top branches of the trees along the crest of the hill. Moonlight spilled broken and silver down the slope. As the moon rose above the trees, the sound of the L&N headed for the tipple drifted up the holler. As a kid, I'd always wanted to slip off and catch that train on the upgrade and ride her all the way to the end of the line. Like Huck Finn, light out for the territories.

Only I'd never had hopped that freight, and now I was too old and tired to run after it. The engineer blew his horn long and low right then and I felt a shudder run through me. A train moaning always has been the lonesomest sound in the world to my way of thinking. At the moment, I didn't need much more lonesome. I ground the stub of my cigarette out against the stone step and whistled for Trips.

3

THE NEXT DAY was Saturday and, even though I'd told myself I'd sleep in, I woke before dawn. A cold front had come through in the night and I shivered as I got dressed. I fired up the stove and started a pot of coffee boiling.

While it was cooking, I went into what had been the parlor when my mother had still been alive and took my shotgun down off the rack. That shotgun had been in my family for three generations. My dad had taught me to hunt with it. I'd cleaned it a few weeks before, but I checked to make sure the barrel wasn't dirty. I got out my old jacket I wore when I went hunting or cutting firewood and filled the pocket with shells. Then I walked back in the kitchen for a breakfast of coffee and cigarettes.

After my second cup, I slipped on my hunting jacket and went out the back door with Trips on my heels. The cool sharpness of the air made me shiver and step out more quickly. Thick fog that had drifted in during the night hung in the pines like cold smoke. I crossed the yard and turned by the tool shed and started up the path that led to the top of the hill.

Sound was muffled that morning. Figured that was due to the fog. I couldn't remember being out in a fog so dense. It was like stepping into a mirage that dampened your face and left spider webs of morning clinging to your hair.

Birds were stirring in the trees, but I couldn't see them. I could hear squirrels squawking, 'course I couldn't see them well enough to shoot. Once, I heard something bigger moving through the undergrowth. Deer, I thought, or maybe a bear. Rumors had been circulating since back in the summer that black bears had returned to this part of Kentucky. In the blind quiet of the morning it was easy to imagine that I was one of the first men to traverse the Cumberland Gap and explore the wilderness that lay west of the Alleghenies. Could have been Daniel Boone or one of his kinsmen, alone in the primeval forests, journeying into unknown territory, keeping an eye out for game, Indians, and the way west.

After ten minutes of steady climbing, I was starting to sweat under my coat. Trips was panting a little as he padded along beside me. The underbrush had thinned out some, and limestone rocks poked through the earth. I went through a cedar thicket and then a stand of old hickory and then I was coming out at the crest of the hill.

The trail curled off to the south, narrowing and running along the crest. After twenty yards or so a mound of rocks had thrust up through the earth forming a sort of chair, or you might call it a throne. When I was a kid there was an old man who lived on the other side of the hill and sometimes I'd climb up the hill and find him seated on the uppermost rock. He wasn't doing much, just sitting there, gazing off in the valley below, or tilting his head and looking up at the sky.

Sometimes he whittled a little, or smoked a corncob pipe. Once I heard him singing. It was a song I'd never heard before and hadn't heard since. A mournful quality ran through that song and an ancient one. Even the words sounded strange and tired as though they were very old and had traveled a long way. I wondered if it was a song from his boyhood.

Most of the time I just waved at him and he nodded at me, although now and then one of us might comment on the weather or pass along a bit of news we'd picked up, like it was a strong piece of string and we were making a gift of it. Last time I saw the old man I'd worked up my nerve and asked him why he sat on the rocks. He looked real solemn for a minute and then he smiled and said in a satisfied way that sitting on the top of that outcropping of stone made him feel closer to God than anywhere else on earth.

Thinking about that old man I climbed up and sat down on the rocks to catch my breath and wait on the fog to lift. It was quiet and peaceful on the rocks and when I closed my eyes it was easy to imagine that maybe God was out there, a swatch of holy smoke drifting in and out of the fog.

After a few minutes, a light breeze began to blow and the fog began to shift and swirl. In a bit, I could see outlines of more rocks and trees and then a patch of sky. Gradually, light began to subdue the fog and the world came into focus. Trips had wandered off among a clump of gnarly, windswept trees and I was all alone. Might have been the only man left on the face of the earth after some plague had taken the others. I was all alone, but, strangely, I wasn't lonely. For the first time I could understand why the old man had come up here so often to sit on the jagged throne of the angels.

**

Before the sun climbed directly overhead I was headed back down the trail. The still warm bodies of two gray squirrels and a rabbit who had zigged when he should have zagged bumped against my leg as they dangled from a rope I'd looped around my belt.

The sun had burned through the fog and the wind had died off and sweat ran down my back and pooled under my arms. My stomach was growling and every few yards Trips would run up and sniff at the squirrels and the rabbit. Cardinals flew in among the pines and once, as I passed through a clearing, I spotted a hawk circling above.

I gutted and skinned the squirrels and the rabbit and picked what lead I could find out of the carcasses. Then, I washed them off with water from the well and carried them inside and cut them up after a ragged fashion. I had a little corn meal saved back in a glass jar and I dumped that out on a plate and coated the meat good. After I got a fire going under a skillet, I spooned in lard and fried up all that meat.

When they were cracklin brown on the outside, I forked them out of the skillet onto a clean plate and carried that over to the table. I ate with my fingers, licking the grease off and now and then tossing a hunk to Trips who was stretched out at my feet giving me the sad eye.

There was a still a bowl full of apples picked out from what was left of Jimmy Hembre's old orchard, and I fingered the one that looked the best. At least it didn't have any bruises or worm holes and I munched on it between bites of squirrel and rabbit.

Trips and I ate all of one squirrel and half the rabbit.

I also ate another hunk of cornbread and tossed Trips a slice of bologna I'd got down at Creekmore's a fortnight before. It smelled all right, but I was afraid that it might be about to go bad.

After I washed up the dishes and swept the floor, I wandered outside and sat in the sun on the stump of an old maple that had gone in a big wind year before last. It was warm in the sun and I got a little drowsy. But before I could doze off a pack of dogs started barking off toward Turner Branch. I listened to them for a while and guessed they were some of Luke Simpson's hounds running a deer or maybe a fox. Luke had good dogs, but he turned pure mean when he took to drinking.

My back got to aching after a bit and I stood up intending to go back inside and see if I could find an old *National Geographic* or maybe a *Field and Stream* to thumb through. Dad had been a reader and never could hardly part with a book or a magazine. Even kept newspapers till Mom used them for a fire or the mice got at them.

As I was walking across the yard, I heard a screen door bang to and I turned and looked down the holler. Figured it was one of the sisters coming out to hang clothes on the line or beat a rug. They were always cleaning at something. But it was old Asa hobbling out on his porch, leaning heavy on his cane. One of his boys, the oldest I think, had carved it for him and he was real proud of that cane. It was pretty, what with birds and butterflies and even a horse's head carved in the hickory. Asa sat down in an old rocker he kept on the porch till the first snow and I turned and walked back in the house.

There was two good hunks of squirrel left and a piece

or three of rabbit and I wrapped them up in a dish towel along with a chunk of cornbread and a few walnuts I'd hulled out the week before and went back out the door and down the path toward the mouth of the holler.

***

"Come on up on the porch, Fast Eddie Burke."

"How'd you know it was me, Asa? I'm only halfway across your yard and I thought you were supposed to be half blind."

He laughed at that; actually it was more of a cackle. "That's only smoke for the womens so I can looks at them and not get in trouble." Asa cackled again. "I'm way too old for trouble."

"You're way too old to be spreading so much molasses around, is what you mean. Hell, there hasn't been a woman on this place in at least five years."

"Now hold on, Fast Eddie. That just ain't true. Why my youngest boy's wife come up with him last Christmas and bought me a chocolate pie." The old man smacked his lips. "Best durn thing I've eat in a blue moon, too. So don't be talking to me about no womens coming here." He paused and cocked his head and looked at me like a suspicious crow, "Why I don't know, Fast Eddie, that a woman ain't come across my threshold since one's come across yours."

I didn't have much to say to that. Fact was, I didn't want to talk about women or my troubles, which in this case were pretty much the same thing. When a woman leaves a man it hurts him bad, scars him down deep, and he's never the same man after that. At least I wasn't. Maybe I'm worse off or better off, but I sure am a different man. Old Asa was sitting back in his rocker grinning at me. For an old man he sure had a mouthful of teeth. I jabbed the dishtowel at him. "Here," I said, "I brought you a little something."

"Well now, I sure do thank you. Let's see what you brought Old Asa." He fumbled with the fold of the dish towel. "Sure does smell good. Yes, I see now, fried squirrel and some nice looking walnuts. Can't remember when I had fried squirrel. How in the world, Fast Eddie, did you know that it is one of my favoritest things in the world to eat?"

I didn't say anything, only grinned back at the old man and wondered how he stood it all day stuck in the little ramshackedly house all by his lonesome.

He folded the towel back and grunted and rocked hard and thrust himself out of the rocking chair. His legs were wobbly and he grabbed hold of one of my arms to steady himself. His grip was surprisingly strong and I wondered how old he was and what sort of life he'd led as a young man.

"Come on," he said, "let's go inside and sit at the table like civilized men."

As we walked slowly across the porch, I wondered what sort of shape I'd be in when I was as old as Asa. At least his wife had never left him. Unless you count dying as leaving, which I guess it was, and about as permanent as it would get.

The floorboards creaked like something alive as I followed him into his kitchen. It was a small room with an old Stokermatic stove in one corner and a small wood-burning cookstove like my Grandma Burke had used in another. One wall was lined with homemade shelves and there were jars of pickles and beans and corn on them.

Canned goods from the A&P in town and a tin of lard and a handful of potatoes covered the bottom shelf. On one of the middle shelves, between a sack of cornmeal and a coffee cup missing a handle, was a framed photograph. While the old man was messing in a drawer, I wandered over and took a look at the photo.

It had been taken on a sunny day. Several people, of varying ages, were standing on a railroad embankment. Behind them was part of a passenger car. All of the people except for one were black. They were all staring into the sun. Their flesh glistened as though the day was hot and sweat had coated their skin.

"What you looking at, Fast Eddie?"

"This old picture you got here next to your cornmeal," I said, turning to face Asa. Late afternoon sunlight was pouring in through a long narrow window and splashing across his face. Asa's right eye looked cloudy and his left one wasn't quite holding still. Maybe he wasn't blind, but for sure he sure couldn't see real clear.

"That one with the train?"

"Yeah, that's the one."

His lips curled up and he nodded his head like I had uttered a profound saying. "That's an old picture, son. See that man in the very front, way over on the left, the one what's got one foot on the rails?"

"I see him."

"Well that was my daddy, Odell, and the woman sort leaning against him, the one what's a-shading her eyes with her hand, why that was my mother, Idalee."

"What about you, Asa? You in this picture?"

"Why sure enough. I'm that little boy clinging to the rail by the door. The one a-hanging off that car like a monkey. And right beside me, a-clinging to the other rail is my cousin, Jefferson Monroe Quince."

I studied the boys closely. Asa's arms didn't look any bigger than a hoe handle, but his eyes glittered in the sunlight like they had been painted on fresh the very morning the photo was taken.

"Never heard you mention anybody of that name," I said, still studying the picture.

I heard the clang of silverware and then a drawer screeching as it closed. "That's 'cause Jefferson Monroe died of the galloping consumption when he was still only a young thing."

The shift in his voice to sadness was as clear as the call of dove on a still morning. "Sorry to hear that," I said.

Asa shuffled toward a small table under the window. He was still holding the food I'd brought him, but now he'd added a stainless steel knife and fork. "Oh, don't be, son, that was a long time ago. So long ago that a whole way of life has done come and gone. So have most of the people." He sat down heavily then lifted his head, a surprised look on his face as though he had just beheld some strange new truth. "Come to think of it, since Mary Robinson died back in the spring, I may be the last one left what had their picture took that day."

"Who's the white man in the photo?"

"That would be Mr. Jim Bernanke. He was the man what hired one of the first group of blacks to come up here to work in his mines and timber. Hired them out of the deep south, Alabama, Mississippi, maybe a few from Louisiana. Don't remember that for sure. Mississippi is where my folks come from."

He closed his eyes and smiled as though he was remembering some sweet days from the long ago. "Down on the Delta, outside a place called Legion Corner, that's where they come from. Where I was born, too. Born in a little two-room shack with cotton growing white on every side and in the summer the days was so hot you thought you was gonna roast like a ear of corn."

"You ever pick cotton?"

"Why sure, even the little babies goes to the cotton fields. Had my own little sack my granny sewed up for me. Course now, I ain't claiming I picked much cotton. Mostly I just drug my sack through that sweet black earth. But yeah, I reckon I picked a little cotton."

He opened his eyes and shook his head, like he was amazed at himself in some strange and wonderful way. "Yes, I've picked cotton and shoveled coal and cut timber and hoed more corn than most men ever saw. Even worked on the railroad for a while, laying track over in Virginia and now I'm an old man, just about all used up."

He fell silent then and I couldn't think of anything to say. The old house went real quiet and after a minute I could hear a bird chirping under the eaves and the creaking of the boards as they settled in the dying afternoon and finally the wind worrying what few leaves remained on a couple of ancient apple trees leaning south at the edge of yard.

I couldn't think of anything to say and I guess Asa couldn't either, or maybe he just wanted to remember something private. Anyway, he didn't say nothing for a long time and I didn't either. After a bit, the thought struck me that maybe we were like those Greeks I'd read about in school, the ones the gods struck blind or deaf or dumb for something they'd done, or something they'd refused to do. Then Asa snorted and laughed and said, "Let's eat us some squirrel meat, boy, and by the way would you mind pouring me a glass of sweet tea out of that pitcher on the counter? Pour yourself one, too, while you're at it." And I nodded and walked over to the cabinet and got two glasses that didn't match down and started pouring.

***

Asa leaned back in his chair and wiped his mouth with a cloth napkin that had faded flowers on it. The napkin looked old and delicate and I wondered if it had belonged to his wife. So much passes, I thought. I turned and looked out the window. The sun had gone behind the hill and the shadows were thick and blue on the scraggly November grass.

"Getting dark out there. Guess I'd better be going."

"Aw, stay awhile, son. You visit so seldom."

"I'll come again."

Asa pushed his chair back and stood up, leaning on the table. He grunted and a moan slipped out between his lips.

"You hurting?'

"No, sir, nothing to speak of. Just old. Been around so long me and Methuselah used run the ridges together. Course I am a sight younger than him." Old Asa grinned at his own humor and scratched the top of this head with one hand.

"Sure," I said, "and you and Moses wandered together in the wilderness for forty years."

"Oh, Lordy, Fast Eddie, I've been wandering in the wilderness for way beyond forty years."

Knowing something about that wandering myself, I nodded and picked up the dishtowel I'd brought the squirrel in.

"Afore you go, son, will you do me one favor?"

"Alright," I said, "if I can. What is it?"

"Like you done ready know, my old eyes ain't what they used to be and I was wondering if you would read me a passage out of the Good Book." The old man plucked his cane from the back of the chair where he'd hung it and started hobbling for what he called the parlor. I let him pass and trailed along. He flopped down on a sofa that sagged fierce in the middle. When he caught his breath, Asa said, "The Good Book's on top of that side table by the door.

"What passage you want me to read?"

"Just open it up and stick your finger on the page and start reading where that finger lands. Been reading that way since I was a little fella. Always figured that was God's way of showing me what he wanted me to hear."

I picked up the Bible. It looked old and was surprisingly heavy. At one time there had been a design of something on the front and it had been outlined in gilt. Over the years, almost all the color had eroded and the outline was very faint. In the fading afternoon sunlight that passed through dirty windows, it was hard to tell what the image was. Might have been an angel or a dove, or maybe even Jesus.

"Just open her up, son, and let the finger of the Lord show you the way."

I opened the Bible at random. Up the holler Trips started barking. Probably a squirrel or a coon. Coons had been coming down off the ridge lately, looking for ears of corns left in the gardens and whatever scraps they could find. The Bible fell open. My finger pressed against a page. The Bible was open to 2 Samuel, Chapter

11, verse 2. I started reading.

"Then it happened one evening that David arose from his bed and walked on the roof of the king's house. And from the roof he saw a woman, and the woman was very beautiful to behold. So David sent and inquired about the woman. And some said, 'Is this not Bathsheba, the daughter of Eliam, the wife of Uriah the Hittite?' Then David sent messengers, and took her; and she came to him, and he lay with her, for she was cleansed from her impurity: and she returned to her house. And the woman conceived; so she sent and told David, and said, 'I am with child.' "

I felt funny reading that sort of stuff to an old man like Asa, but he was sitting on the couch nodding like it was all making good sense to him. Figured he'd probably read the Bible cover to cover, so I swallowed and kept on reading about how David had Bathsheba's husband, Uriah the Hittite, get out in front of the army in a battle and, of course, the poor fool was killed. Bathsheba ended up moving in with David and having a son and I guess they were pleased about that, but the last line I read was scary. "But the thing that David had done displeased the Lord." Even though I wasn't any sort of a regular church goer, I knew that verse was prophesying bad times for David. My voice trailed off after that last verse and I let the Bible close.

"I thank you kindly, sir, for reading the Holy Word to me, and for the good meat. You have nourished me body and soul."

"You're welcome," I said and placed the Bible back on the side table. A strange feeling was washing through me, as though reading those words had hollowed me out. Bible verses always spooked me.

Not knowing why I did it, I walked across the worn linoleum and shook the old man's hand. Arthritis had got a grip on him and his bones and knuckles protruded at odd angles. I shook his hand gently. Then, I picked up the towel and turned and went out the door and into the thickening dusk. As the door closed, I heard the old man say "Good-night," but I didn't know what to say, so I just went down the steps and out into the yard.

The air was going dark now and had a purplish cast to it and the path was hard to see. I found it though and bent my neck and trudged on up the hill, suddenly as tired as though I'd done a day's work. Even a little religion can be right hard on a man. Halfway to my house, I could hear my dog barking and when I looked up the moon was peeking through the tops of the pines.

Snapshot

4

TURP LAWSON'S HOUSE stood on a shelf of rock that jutted out over a valley that didn't have any particular name. I wasn't for sure, but it seemed to me that one or maybe two of Oscar McComb's boys lived in that valley. When I was a kid I used to fish Pumpkin Creek, which wandered around that valley, with my cousin Jarred Lester. Course that was before I ever knew Karen.

Turp hadn't said for sure what time I was supposed to show up and I had no idea when they ate, so I waited till the sun was considerable past its zenith and started walking. Must have taken almost an hour of steady walking before I saw the Lawson place. It wasn't much, just a squared off shack built out of green lumber. As I came down the path, I could see a couple of the boards had already started to warp.

Turp, or somebody, had run a length of clothesline between a couple of handmade posts and there was a pile of rocks beside the house that reminded me of something, although I wasn't sure what. Curtains hung in the window and on the front door there was a wreath made out of wild grape vines and maple leaves. The place sure had a woman's touch. At one time so had mine, I thought as I walked across the pebbly yard. Stepping up onto the porch, I realized that I'd been missing that touch without even knowing.

Before I could knock on the door, it swung open and

Turp Lawson motioned me on inside. He was a big one for shaking hands, which I didn't much care for, especially since it was only Turp. But, since I was eating with the man, I shook his hand.

A woman came out of another room and she was smiling. I'd never seen her before. Her hair was golden and shining and it curled around her face like a cap. She stood at the edge of the room, leaning against the wall, one foot tucked behind the other, with her head lowered in a shy looking way, eying me up through her lashes.

Way she was looking at me gave me a funny feeling, although I couldn't say why for sure. I had a little flower vase full of beautyberry stems with berries. It hadn't seem right showing up with nothing and the little blue vase was only a cheap thing that Karen had left behind. Turp was blabbering about how glad he was to see me and all, but I just kept on walking and crossed the floor and handed the woman the vase. "Here," I said, "this is for you. For going to so much trouble and all."

She smiled then and took the vase out of my hand and looked at it real hard. The woman had a way of staring at something that made you wonder if she was quite right. But her face was kind of pretty, if you didn't like them thin, and she had a figure that sure caught your eye.

"Those berries are right pretty. Did you cut those branches for me?"

"Thought they were a pretty color, maybe cheer up the house some."

I felt a hand on my shoulder and then out of the corner of my eye I could see Turp's face. He was so close that the side of his face was blurry. Being so close, he made me a little nervous.

Snapshot

"Marta, this is Eddie Burke, the man I told you about. The one who's come to eat with us today. I work with Eddie."

"Oh, yeah, I remember. Nice to meet you, Eddie."

"Nice to meet you, Mrs. Lawson."

"Just call me Marta."

Turp patted my shoulder. "Yeah, Eddie, call her Marta."

I nodded and Turp started talking about what all we were going to eat and shooing us into another room. Marta walked on ahead of us. The next room was a bigger than usual kitchen with a good-sized table in front of a window. The table looked like it had been made out of oak. Marta sat the vase of berries in the center of the table and Turp had us all sit down. Then he said grace, but while he was praying I was staring out the window at the land sloping off toward the valley below, wishing I wasn't here. It felt strange sitting down to eat with Turp and his wife.

I hadn't been so close to a woman in a long time. And this one smelled nice, like spring flowers, and now and then, when I wasn't staring out at the gum and the sugar maples and the birds circling above the valley floor, I was sneaking a peek at her. Once our eyes met and she smiled real polite like, which made me sort of ashamed and sort of something else.

Turp finally finished praying and he paused and lifted his head up and looked at me. I had the feeling that I was supposed to say or do something, but my mind was blank. After a minute I nodded and said, "Amen."

That goofy grin of his spread all over Turp's face and he looked over at his wife and said, "Pass the potatoes, will you, hon?"

It didn't take more than a glance to see that Turp's wife had done a lot of cooking. Beside the fried potatoes, there was ham and shucky beans and cornbread and fried apples and a big bowl of soup beans, still steaming. And at the far end of the table was a dried apple stack cake.

"Have some fried taters, Eddie."

I'd been lost looking at all that food and Turp's voice startled me. Hadn't seen so much food in one place since that last Christmas when Mom was still living.

I took the bowl and spooned a few out on my plate. As soon as I'd passed the bowl to Marta, Turp was handing me the ham. The dishes kept on coming around and all the time Turp was telling some story about a traveling man who had got lost over in Knott County and run off a cliff. I never did get straight whether the man was from Ohio or Indiana, or even whether he lived or died in the crash. Turp's wife was sitting across the table, nibbling a little now and again, but mostly looking at her husband and laughing every little bit. Like I said, I wasn't following the story real close, but it seemed to me she was laughing in the wrong places.

About halfway through the tale, just as I'd stuffed a piece of ham in my mouth, I felt something rub across the top of my right boot. At first I thought it was a mouse. They'll always try to get inside when the weather starts turning cold. But then whatever it was rubbed across the top of my boot again, only slower this time, and I could feel more weight than any mouse ever carried.

My next thought was that it was Turp acting the fool. He did that some at the mine. Only when I looked his way, he was just grinning with that goofy grin of his and starting in on the weather. The way he was turned in his seat I could tell that it wasn't his foot that had been rubbing. That left only one answer to that question and I didn't want to face up to it, at least not right then, so I just stared down at my plate and chewed the ham to shreds.

"Well, Eddie, what do you think?"

I swallowed what I was chewing. "What's that, Turp? Sorry, but my mind was wandering."

"I was just asking if you thought the other fellows would mind if I joined you next Friday night."

"Oh, you mean J.D. and Lonnie? I'll ask. Usually they don't mind. Only you'll need to bring your own liquor. Ever' man supplies his own, if you know what I mean. Less you've got enough to share."

"Oh, I'll have a plenty to share. Junior Miller's boy is gonna cut me a real good deal on account of this will be my first time buying from him and I reckon he wants me to keep coming back."

I forked some fried potatoes in my mouth and chewed on them while I thought what to say. I swallowed and wiped my mouth with one of the cloth napkins Marta had put out. "Like I told you before, Turp, you can buy from whoever you want to, but I've heard bad stories about that shine Speck Jr. sells. "

"Ah, it'll be alright. I've known Junior pert near all my life. He's okay, people just don't know how to take him sometimes."

I started to say something, but just then something rubbed up under one leg of my trousers and I could feel my face getting all hot, so I bent down low over my plate and poked a little at some beans. Then, real slow like, so as not to startle anyone, I pulled both legs back behind me and wrapped them around the legs of my chair.

Marta leaned forward in her chair, her head swung out over the table. "Turp can't hold his liquor."

"Hesh, Marta," Turp said, his voice rising.

I didn't know what to say. I felt embarrassed for all of us. It wasn't comfortable sitting with my legs all wrapped up like that, so I straightened them out.

"Every time he takes a drink or two, he gets all affectionate and after he gets three or four slugs down, why he turns mean, or else real sad."

"Thanksgiving's a-comin up," Turp said real quick like when Marta paused for breath. She was rubbing my foot again. That bothered me. Bothered me in any number of ways. I'd been alone way too long.

"Yeah," I said, "what is it, three or four weeks?"

Marta opened her eyes real wide. They were the color of wet coal. They were staring at me.

"What's your name, again, mister?"

"Eddie."

"You're a pretty man, Eddie."

I felt my face go red. "Guess, I'd better head for the house. Got to work tomorrow."

"Turp ain't a pretty man, like you."

"Be quiet, Marta. Don't talk silly. Eddie don't want to hear your mouth a-runnin." Turp turned to me and said out of the side of his mouth, "Don't pay no attention to what she says, Eddie, Marta just gets to talking silly sometimes."

I nodded and tried to focus on the world outside.

"Get me and Eddie a piece of cake, Marta. My wife makes the best dried apple stack cake you'll ever eat. She's a real good cook."

"Everything tasted good," I said.

"She'll be cooking a big old turkey for Thanksgiving,

maybe you can join us."

"Little early to know what I'll be doing," I said, wondering where Turp was going to get a turkey.

As if he was reading my mind, he said, "Her daddy owns the A&P over to Hazard. Said he'll fix us up with a hen turkey and all the trimmings."

A shadow fell across my plate and then something soft was rubbing against my shoulder. Marta slid a big piece of cake on a clean saucer in front of me. Her fingertips brushed against the side of my face that was turned away from Turp. I concentrated on that piece of cake while she strolled over and gave Turp a piece. It eased my mind some to see that his piece of cake was as big as mine.

I could smell the apples and the flour. Something else lingered in the air. It was the fragrance of violets. Perfume sure gets a man's attention. Karen had always liked perfume that smelled of roses. I set my mind to eating my cake and slipping out first chance I got. All manner of emotions were whirling around inside of me, and some of them weren't proper, and I didn't totally trust myself.

Turp and his wife were arguing a little now, something about one of her brothers who Turp had had words with. A crow was calling somewhere just over the ridge line. I could hear his rusty old voice, and I tried to concentrate on his caw-caw-caw. That sound and the cake in my mouth. Only the cake was dry and had a musty taste like it had been made with old flour and I'd never been much of a stack cake man anyway. Berry pies were more my line. Blackberry, especially. I could still remember picking blackberries when I was a kid. Seemed like they got ripe just at the hottest, most muggy time of summer and their thorns would prick you till blood ran down the tips of your fingers and the chiggers would dig into your hide so that no amount of scratching was any real help. Worst of all was the worry about snakes. Snakes just seemed to love to curl up underneath a blackberry bush. Guess they liked the shade. Or maybe they'd figured the thorns would protect them. Who knew what went on inside a snake's brain.

After a while I quit thinking about snakes and got to thinking about Marta, most especially her breasts. The way they pushed out against her dress sure grabbed a man's attention. Seemed like I just couldn't quit thinking about them. Karen's breasts had been small, although her nipples had been big and dark, sort of like blackberries starting to ripen. What with snakes and the temptation of Marta's breasts I was getting all mixed up in my mind. I decided to head home at the first opportunity.

All the time I'd been crawling around inside my mind Turp and his wife had been going at it. Even with that she kept rubbing the top of my shoe. Someway she'd gotten her shoe off and her foot was warm when she pushed it up inside the legs of my pants. Hadn't had a woman touch me like that in a long time. Finally, something Turp said rubbed her the wrong way and she tossed her napkin down and in a minute she stood up and stomped off toward the kitchen. In a bit I could hear the rattling pans.

"Guess, I'd be going," I said and pushed my chair back.

"No need to rush off."

"I'm not rushing, but I've got a goodly walk ahead of me."

Turp nodded and pushed his chair back. "Glad you

could make it. Come on, I'll walk you to the door." As I followed him I wondered what I should say. He swung the door open and stepped out on the porch. Floorboards groaned under his weight.

The sun was already down amongst the tree tops and the air was sharply cooler. Just like I figured he would, Turp stuck out his hand. Shaking it made me feel funny, I mean after the way his wife had been rubbing on me it didn't seem a natural thing to do.

"Thanks for the meal. Tell your wife I really enjoyed it."

"I'll do it." He let go of my hand. "Don't pay no attention to what she says. Marta's a good woman, but sometimes she gets a little mixed up. In her mind, I mean. See, she had some kind of fever when she was thirteen and ever since then, well, she takes spells where she says the first wild thing that comes to her mind. Crazy stuff, you know. Tales about ghosts and dogs with two heads and trees a growing leaves on New Year's Day. Crazy stuff. Why last month she went on for a week about Joe Henry Johnston. You know Joe Henry?"

"Heard of him."

"Well, anyway she was convinced that he was in love with her. Claimed he tried to kiss her after Sunday night services and wrote her love notes. 'Course she couldn't produce any notes like that 'cause he never wrote 'em. Don't believe anybody who is friends with a man, who eats his food and such, would make a pass at his wife. Not unless they was a like a snake let loose in the Garden of Eden. Don't you agree?"

"Sure, that's right," I said thinking that Turp was laying it on kind of thick. But maybe if I'd done that I'd be walking back home holding hands with my wife. Anyway, I'd played that game another way and made a proper mess of it.

I looked off toward the timber and just then a crow flapped his wings and rose off the lower limb of a black oak like demons was after him. Old people were always saying something about crows flying at sundown being an omen, but I couldn't remember if it was a good omen or a bad one. "Well, thanks again. See you tomorrow," I said and stepped off the porch and went down the steps and out in the yard before Turp could start in again. I already had plenty to think about.

I was halfway across the cut grass when he hollered after me. "You won't forget now will you?"

I stopped and turned halfway around. "Forget what?"

"To ask J.D. and Lonnie about next weekend. You know, getting together and drinking and all."

"No, I won't forget. See ya," I said and flung up a hand and turned and walked at a good pace for the timber. The sun had turned the color of hot blood off to the west and I could hear the crow cawing deep in the darkening woods. At the edge of the tree line I turned and looked back. A face shone in the window. Yellow hair glowed against the thickening dusk.

5

ON MONDAY, I thought about her most of the day and tried to work away from Turp Lawson. On Tuesday, I thought about her the way man thinks about a brand new Cadillac, beautiful, but something I'd never have.

Since Mom died I hadn't set a foot inside a church, except to marry Karen and I didn't think that counted as worshiping the Lord. Still, when I was little Mom had made the whole family go to church, at least most Sundays. Although Dad had gone mainly at Easter and Christmas, or whenever there was an accident at the mine. Anyway, I was Christian enough to know that lusting after another man's wife was wrong. That bothered me, but not enough to keep from lusting.

Mom had always kept a Bible in the house. She'd called it the Holy Book. By Tuesday night my conscience had got to bothering me enough that I hunted around until I found it. For some reason somebody had stuck it under the bed beneath Dad's old collection of arrowheads.

I drug it out and dusted it off and searched until I found the verse I was looking for. It was in Exodus. It was the tenth commandment. I read it seven times. 'You shall not covet your neighbor's house, you shall not covet your neighbor's wife, nor his manservant, nor his maidservant, nor his ox, nor his donkey, nor anything that is your neighbor's."

Now, Turp wasn't exactly my neighbor. That would have been Asa, or maybe the Davis sisters. But he didn't live that far away and anyway I knew how a preacher would interpret that verse. Even when I lay down and closed my eyes and tried to dream about something nice, I kept hearing the words of that commandment. Only it wasn't God saying them, or Moses, or even Billy Riley who taught school during the week to pay the bills and preached Hell and Salvation on Sunday down at the Mountain Holiness church. The voice I was hearing was Turp Lawson's and that voice made my nerves sing like a plucked guitar string. Sleep didn't come till way after midnight and when it did it was a restless, disturbed sleep. A sleep like I had a fever, which I guess maybe I did.

Warm winds started blowing just after daylight on Wednesday, rattling the window glass and sending a golden shower of ginkgo leaves spiraling toward the earth. By the time I could see the mouth of the mine it was starting to sprinkle.

We were working in bad coal that day. There was all kinds of slag and the roof bolts kept groaning until it made a man so nervous he had one eye on the roof and one on the seam he was working in. One of the cutting machines broke down and Joe Perry and one of the Grissom boys almost came to blows. I was glad when Joe Cox, who was foreman, hollered that it was time for lunch.

J.D. and Lonnie and me found us a room off the main where nobody was working and got our backs up against a wall and opened our lunch buckets. I didn't have much, some cornbread, which was going dry and I was right tired of, a slice of ham Turp had given me on

Sunday, and few raisins I'd found in a box in the pantry. They tasted only a little old. J.D. had a big old meatloaf sandwich and a hunk of dried apple pie, while Lonnie had two bologna sandwiches and some pickles his wife had made back in the summer. Lonnie's wife only had one good eye, but she was supposed to be the best cook this side of Whitesburg.

J.D. and Lonnie was talking about basketball and I ate my ham and raisins and listened to them and wondered if it was still raining outside and what Marta was doing. Only all the time I was feeling sorta guilty for thinking about Marta some and for not having asked about Friday night for Turp.

After a bit J.D. and Lonnie quit talking and concentrated on eating. I got up my nerve.

"You guys know Turp Lawson?"

"Heard of him," J.D. said.

"He that skinny guy that acts kind of goofy?"

"Yeah, that's him. Lives over on the other side of the ridge."

"I've seen him around," Lonnie said. "What about him?"

"Well, I don't how he found out about our Friday nights, but he wants to join us and do a little drinking."

J.D. made a face, but didn't say anything. Lonnie looked at me over the top of a bologna sandwich. "He ain't much to look at. Know anything about him?"

"Not much," I said, "but he and his wife had me over for Sunday dinner."

"Turp Lawson is married?" Lonnie sounded real surprised.

"Yeah, but I don't know his wife." I was sorta pleased with myself for sticking pretty closely to the truth.

Lonnie looked over at J.D., but J.D. only shrugged. Lonnie turned his head back around and peered down his nose at me. "Well, I guess it would be okay the once, but he's got to bring his own liquor."

"Oh, he promised he would," I said. "I'll let him know."

J.D. nodded and Lonnie went back to working on his bologna and white bread.

***

The feeling that Turp would be looking for me after work had been tickling the back of my brain all day, so I wasn't surprised when he hollered my name coming out of the mine.

I was about twenty yards ahead of him and I turned and stepped back under the drooping branches of a big old spruce tree that grew between the road and a shelf of limestone that protruded from the side of the hill. The sky was raining harder now and the wind had shifted so that it was coming out of the west. There was a chill in that west wind and the limestone glittered where it had been washed clean by the rain.

"Well," Turp said as he came up, "did you ask 'em yet?"

"Everything's set."

"Friday night?"

"That's right," I said, scrunching up my neck. Rain water was dripping down the back of my shirt.

Turp wiped at his face. You could hear the rain peppering down now against the rocks and the bare earth and the fallen leaves. You could almost smell the seasons changing.

"What time do you all meet up?"

I peered over his shoulder and down the slope and then off across the valley. Rain shimmered above the trees and the houses and the people like an alive curtain. Part of me wanted to take all my clothes off and let that shimmering rain wash me clean. Only deep down I knew there were stains that no rain could wash away.

"No particular time," I said. "We just all buy whatever we aim to drink and then we meet up at the cabin."

Turp nodded. He was wearing an old ball cap, but he had it pushed up and his nose protruded beyond the short rim and the tip of it was wet. "Now, where precisely is that cabin?"

"Just a little ways down on Gover Creek, about fifty yards past the old school house, or what's left of it. Tom Sizemore lived there afore he died. Know where it is?"

"Close enough," Turp said. "I'll find it."

"Well," I said, "see you then for sure." I glanced up at the lead gray sky. "Guess I'll head for the house 'for I get any wetter."

"You're welcome to come over and sit a spell," Turp said. "Marta's gone to spend the night at her aunt's house over by Beverly."

"Thanks," I said, "but think I'll take it to the house."

"Alright. I'll see you Friday evening."

"Don't forget your liquor," I said over my shoulder.

"I won't," he said and I raised a hand and kept walking. Just at the bend I took a quick look back. Turp was still standing in the rain. He looked dark and lonesome, putting me in mind of a pine tree.

***

By the time I made the mouth of the holler the rain had given way to a fine mist that hung so low to the ground that it was like walking through a cloud. Droplets of water fell from the leaves that remained on the trees and from the bill of my cap and gathered on the ground in small puddles like tidal pools I remembered reading about when I was in school.

All sound was muffled by the mist. My own footsteps sounded like they were falling some distance away and the call of a jaybird might have come from anywhere. Usually, I could hear Trips barking by now, but there was only the drip of rain on fallen leaves and the muffled thud of my footsteps.

Light glowed in Asa's front window and though I couldn't see his face I waved anyway. The Davis sisters' house was dark and I figured they'd gone visiting. They had any number of cousins who lived over around Washoe and the ridges beyond.

At first I thought it was just a trick of the light. It was just going dusk and at that time of day the light can be deceitful. Halfway up the slope, I figured it was a light I'd left burning and I cursed. Ten steps later I could see that the light was outside and then I could see that it was a head of golden hair, dampened by the mist and curling around a face I knew.

She stood up as I came across the yard. She was smiling. "Surprised to see me?"

"Very," I said. "Turp thinks you're spending the night with your aunt."

"I know, that's what I told him. He always believes me. He can be so dumb."

"He's gonna be so mad when he finds out what you've done."

She reached out and touched my hand and pushed her face real close to mine, smiling all the time. "How's he ever gonna find out, Eddie? I ain't a-tellin nothing, are you?"

For a moment, I simply stood there, wondering about Trips for some strange reason. Usually, he was home to greet me, but sometimes he got to chasing a rabbit or a deer and might not come home till way after dark, almost too tired to bark and hungry enough to eat a bag of railroad spikes.

Then the wind shifted, blowing cool across the back of my neck, and I suddenly felt all exposed, like the whole world was watching us. Of course it wasn't, only a fox or a squirrel, or maybe some bird huddled up in a pine tree trying to get out of the damp. Asa was too blind to see all the way from the mouth of the holler and the sisters were gone, but still I felt exposed. "Let's go inside," I said, "it's getting cold and dark and I'm tired."

It was strange seeing a woman in the kitchen. She shook her wet hair like a dog does. There were some old towels stacked up in a corner of the bedroom and I went and got one for her and one for me. I didn't aim to, but I watched her drying off. Ways she moved did things to me.

The last part of her body she dried was her face. She bent her neck and rubbed her face in the towel and came up grinning. For the first time, I really noticed her teeth. They were big, but they looked clean.

"Wanna see my titties?"

I just didn't know what to say. I mean I did and I didn't. I just kept my mouth shut and stared at her. Without another word, she tugged her sweater over her head and quicker than I could have imagined, she had undone her bra. Her breasts swung free, round and soft-looking and pale as milk except for her nipples. They were the pink of peach petals, and stiff.

"Come on, Eddie, you can kiss them. You know you want to."

I had to swallow real hard to get any words out. "But you're a married woman."

"So," she whispered, running one finger down the side of my face. I could hear the stubble rustle. "Turp, he ain't no good in bed. Got himself just a tiny little thing, like a little boy and even that he can't get good and hard."

I didn't want to hear her talk that way anymore. I was embarrassed for Turp and for her and for me. Knew I should say something. What I was thinking was wrong. Even the Bible said so. Only thing to do was make her get dressed and go home. Lust was a sin according to the Bible. Lusting after the wife of a man you worked with seemed about as bad as it could get. Just by standing there and doing nothing I was committing a sin.

"Ain't I pretty, Eddie?"

I nodded.

"And you're a pretty man, too. I like pretty things, don't you?"

"Sure," I said, my voice kind of squeaky, "Guess everybody likes pretty things."

Marta pressed her head against my chest. I could feel her fingers fumbling with my buttons. She smelled like damp violets. Her body was very soft. Want rose in my throat until it formed a knot I couldn't swallow.

"Kiss me, Eddie."

"I shouldn't."

"Kiss me, honey, please."

I told myself no. I tell myself lots of things.

She had lips that were made for kissing and her body was soft and warm and rubbing me in all the sensitive places. "Eddie?"

"What?"

"Let's go make a baby. I want a baby so bad. I've wanted one since I was a little girl. Let's go make us a pretty baby. Me and you is pretty people and our baby would just naturally be pretty. Come on, Eddie," she said, and all the time her fingers and lips were working on me. Knowing it was wrong, I bent and got my arms around her and scooped her up. She was heavier than I'd guessed, but that didn't matter. Nothing much mattered right then.

As I eased her down on the bed, I could hear the wind whining up under the eaves and the rain had started up again and was pecking against the glass trying to get in. The room was dark but her hair was gold and her lips were warm and it had been a very long time. Before long I forgot to remember about sinning. I said her name like it was a psalm.

***

I woke deep in the night, sweating, heart pounding as though I'd been running. A vein throbbed in one temple and my head ached the way mother always allowed hers did during one of her spells.

For some time I just lay there, listening to the rain on the roof and Marta breathing and the wind worrying at the window glass. No one had slept in the house but me since Karen had left and, one way or another, she'd been gone a good long time. In one way it was peaceful, but in another it was troublesome. I had some answering to do and I knew it. If not to Turp Lawson, then to God. Neither encounter promised to be pleasant. After a while the wind began to die off and my mind started to settle down. Just at the edge of sleep I heard Trips whining at the back door.

I eased the quilt back and slipped out of bed. A chill had filled the room and I shivered as I slipped on my shirt and jeans. I padded barefoot to the back door, carrying my boots and socks with me.

Trips was wet and shivering and blood was dripping from a long cut on his nose. I grabbed an old rag and wiped at the blood. The cut was long, but not deep. As I dried him off, I wondered who he had been scrapping with.

The window in the kitchen needed caulking and I could feel the chilly air seeping in around the frame. Caulking was another of those jobs I was always putting off. I got up and put out food and water for Trips. After that, I poked at the embers in the Warm Morning and added kindling and a couple of pieces of old newspaper, twisted up tight. When I had the fire going good, I got down the bottle of Four Roses I kept hid back for special occasions and poured myself a healthy shot. Then, I sat down at the table. Sat there for a long time, sipping on whiskey, nibbling on my walnut stash, and thinking about what I'd done and what needed doing. Trips padded over and settled down against me. I rubbed his head and scratched behind his ears and pretty soon he dozed off.

Never did go back to sleep myself, even with two generous shots of the good stuff. Instead, I only considered what I'd gone and gotten myself into. Except for a little while, just before daylight, when I tried to pray. Only I was out of practice and the prayer never said what I aimed for it to. When the light outside started to change I put on my boots and grabbed my coat.

Before I went out the back door I tiptoed back in the bedroom and kissed Marta. She was on her back and one shoulder gleamed bare. She was snoring gently.

6

TURP LAWSON DAMN NEAR scared the piss out of me. I'd been hiding out from him for two days and it was almost quitting time on Friday. For about the last ten minutes I'd been shooting the bull with Boyd Fowler while he was working on a cutting machine that had broke down right after lunch. Boyd had been off in a rough room they just shot that morning and as I was rounding the corner, headed toward the mantrip, I ran smack into Turp Lawson.

"There you are," he said, "been looking for you all day."

"Just been plugging away."

Turp leaned forward, so close now that I could smell tobacco on his breath. "We're still on for tonight, ain't we?"

"Far as I know," I said.

"Tom Sizemore's old place?"

"That's it."

"What time?"

"No special time," I said, "everybody just sorta shows up after they get their liquor." I forced myself to look at Turp. He was trembling a little, the way leaves on a river birch will in a breeze. Plus, there was a glitter to his eyes that put in mind of some kind of animal. Turp Lawson made me nervous. Course, part of that might have been my conscience bothering me.

"Must be about quitting time," I said. "Guess we ought to get a move on."

"'Kay," he said, and clapped me on the shoulder, "see you tonight, buddy."

I had to swallow hard, twice, before I could spit out, "See ya."

Afore he could say anything more, I stepped on around him and hustled toward the mantrip. This one was crowded, but I elbowed in between Johnny White and Artho Fannin. As soon as we started moving the tension began draining out of me. By the time I could see daylight I was as limp as a wet noodle.

Eller Whitman, who owned the mine, always showed up on the Fridays we got our pay. Oh, he was around a lot others times too, but paydays you could rely on him showing up just like you could daylight coming. He always asked after a man's family or inquired how the day had gone. If a miner got hurt, he sent around canned goods or a ham and he was good to visit the sick. What impressed me the most was how when some member of a miner's family passed, Mr. Whitman was always at the funeral, right next to the miner, with one arm across the shoulders of the grieving. To me, that said a lot about the man.

I got in line behind Tommy Renfro and we talked about how cold it was turning and how his kids was doing in school this year. Tommy was a good guy, but he had a hard row to hoe. Back in the spring, a big slab of jackrock fell on his right foot and broke three bones. He missed a lot of work with that and then, just when he was catching up a little, his wife came down with walking pneumonia. Word was her doctor bills were something fierce.

What with Mr. Whitman saying a few words to every man, it took awhile to get to the front of the pay line. My legs were tired and my head was starting to ache by the time Tommy signed for his paycheck and headed for home.

"Turning winter on us isn't it, Eddie?"

"Yes, sir," I said. Mr. Whitman had extended his hand and I reached out and shook it. Like I said, Mr. Whitman spoke to every man. Knew us all by name. Plus, he always seemed ready to shake a man's hand. Gave a fellow a good feeling to work for a man like Eller Whitman.

"How are things up the holler?"

"Alright, I reckon," I said, thinking for just a moment that somehow Mr. Whitman had found out about me and Marta. I didn't know whether Mr. Whitman was a church-going man or not, but I didn't think he'd care for one of his workers messing around with the wife of another.

"Seen my old friend, Asa Washington, lately?

"Why sure," I said. "Was just down at his house the other evening. Didn't know you knew Asa."

"Sure, I know Asa. He used to cut timber for my dad when I was a kid and now and then I'd go fishing for cats with him down on the Kentucky. Used to catch some big ones, too."

"Well, well, I sure never knew that."

Mr. Whitman laughed. "Dare say there's lots about both me and Asa you don't know. Now I can't speak for Asa, but I don't aim to tell too much on myself." And he grinned real big and with that grin and his smooth combed white hair and that fine big coat he wore, why he just looked like someone on the cover of one of those slick magazines.

Just to be sociable, I grinned, too, and he handed me a paycheck and said, "Guess you're looking for this?" I nodded and shook his hand again before I signed the paybook. Now, it would have been pleasant to stand and chat some more with him, but there were other tired, hungry men behind me and the wind was starting to bite and the taste of the whiskey was already filling my mouth. So, I mumbled "Thanks" and bent into that icy wind.

***

The only place to get a check cashed so late in the day on Friday was Sam Creekmore's liquor store and it was almost three miles from the bottom of the hill. My best shot was to catch a ride. Last light clung to the sky off toward Lexington. I hustled on down the hill.

Buddy Collett's truck was just backing out of his parking place when I came around the last stand of pine and I started running and flagged him down before he got on the road. Buddy was a distant cousin on my mom's side and he carried me all the way to Sam's.

Sam was behind the counter as usual and his two boys was both sitting on stools letting their pistols show. Sam aimed to avoid trouble if he could, but he wasn't going to hesitate to stop a man from stealing from him. Before he had the boys hang around on paydays, he'd been robbed twice and the last time somebody cracked him over the head with a tire iron. Most of the local men were good fellows, but now and then one got drunk and forgot his raising. Plus, sometimes carloads would come in from Perry or Floyd County and once a real bunch of hell-raisers drove over from West Virginia.

I cashed my check and bought a bologna sandwich, a pint of Old Yellowstone, and a pack of Camels. I didn't buy a lot of smokes, but I figured puffing on a coffin nail every now and then couldn't hurt much. Sam gave me back my change and we talked for a few minutes while I ate my sandwich about the weather and the price of coal and the way Congress was acting stupid. Surprised me a little how hungry I was and I ordered another sandwich, cheese this time, and ate that, too.

I was full and starting to get antsy when a couple of the Jones boys from up Tricky Creek came through the door and started yakking at Sam, so I just put my smokes in my shirt pocket and slipped my pint down inside my coat and headed for the door. I nodded at one of Sam's boys on the way out. Think it was Jim Wayne.

Outside it had gone hard dark and the only light was what spilled from the windows of the store and headlights that happened to be passing. Once I got out of the arc of the lights, I eased off into the tree line and took off one boot and stuffed my grocery money all the way down in the toe. One lesson I'd learned the hard way was not to make it too easy to get to your money when you started drinking. Slim pickings gets real tiresome after a few days.

The old house where we did our drinking wasn't all that far and I was glad, 'cause by now that wind was like a knife of ice. To fortify myself, I took a good slug of whiskey and lit up a cigarette. Then I crossed the parking lot and turned left.

Clouds had the sky smothered and it was powerful dark walking down the road. The county had paved it the year before, but because of the hillside there really wasn't room for shoulders and it was chancy every time I had to step off when a car came. Still, traffic wasn't heavy and I moved along good and before I cut over the hill by the old Pentecostal Church I'd started to sweat under my coat and workshirt.

Once I dropped down off the highway, the road was gravel for a while and then nothing more than a path of beaten earth all the way to the abandoned house. But it ran under a cutbank and pines and cedars and hickory and burr oaks grew real thick and close to the trail so that the wind wasn't bothersome anymore.

It was so dark among those trees that I could barely see my own hand in front of me. I wished the clouds would break and let the moon shine on through, but they held on and I stumbled twice, only one of them wasn't much.

Walking along that dark trail and hearing rustling in the leaves and once the cry of some night bird, I started to get the feeling that I was the only man on earth, or at least I was experiencing what some of the pioneers did when they first come through the Cumberland Gap and started searching out Kentucky. In one way that was a lonesome feeling, but, in another, it brought a peace to my mind. Anyway, I just slogged along in the dark, stopping once to take a leak and once to take a hit off my bottle, wondering if Turp would show and if he suspicioned anything and what I would do if he did. All that wondering got my head to hurting again and for more than one reason I was glad to see a light burning in the old ramshackedly house.

All three of them were already there. Guess up to the minute I pushed open the door I expected Turp to not show. But he was there, sitting in the corner, drinking something out of a Mason jar that looked like slightly cloudy spring water. His checks were already flushed and there was a good inch between the top of the jar and the surface of the shine.

J.D. and Lonnie were there, too, but I'd expected them. I'd seen Lonnie's banged-up Ford at the gravel pull-off. He and J.D. lived close to each other and lots of times they shared a ride. When he could, J.D. kicked in some on gas. J.D. was puffing on a cig and Lonnie was trying to make music out of a harmonica he'd ordered back in the summer from Montgomery-Ward.

"Well, look what the wind done blowed in," J.D. said around the cigarette.

Lonnie nodded and kept on playing. It was a snatch of a tune he'd been working on for weeks.

"Hey," I said and rubbed my hands together, realizing suddenly how cold I was. I figured Turp would say something, probably something silly, but he only smiled like he was real shy and took another sip.

J.D. blew smoke out his nose. "You get lost, Eddie?"

"No, just chatting some with Sam up to the store."

Lonnie pulled the harmonica away from his lips and banged the spit out. "Cold out there, ain't it?"

" 'Most winter," I said.

"Well, pull up a chair and sit a spell," J.D. said and pulled a glass half-pint out of his coat pocket.

He was only joshing about the chair because there wasn't a stick of furniture in the place. What the scavengers hadn't got we'd burnt up staying warm last January. The other three were sitting in corners, like they'd claimed territory, so I crossed the squeaky floor and sat down in the empty corner. J.D. lifted his bottle. Light from the kerosene lamp glittered off it and made it look like a valuable jewel. "Cheers."

"Bottoms up," Lonnie said. Real casual like, I looked over at Turp, wondering what he would say. Only he didn't say a word, just raised his Mason jar. Seemed like a good response to me, so I screwed the cap off my bottle. Then we all nodded at each other and took a good slug. The whiskey burned going down, but it had hardly hit my stomach before I felt the warmth start to spread. I took another hit, just a sip this time and closed my eyes. It had been a long week and even my bones ached and the whiskey seemed to push all the cold and tiredness and worries off into the darkness. Maybe that's why a man drank a little on the weekends, I thought. He needed that peaceful relief to get him through the week.

J.D. said something about a dance in town on Saturday and Lonnie answered that the last two times he'd been he'd gotten in a fight so he wasn't going. Then they got to talking about cars. J.D. was always going to buy a car and Lonnie was always talking about getting a new one. J.D. was a Chevy man and Lonnie thought nothing was as dependable as a Ford. But it was all talk. Lonnie's old bomb only ran about half the time and J.D. wasn't going to buy any car. Not with three kids at home and another on the way. Just talk. That's all it was. That's all ninety percent of our blabbing was. We were just talking to make ourselves look good, or excuse some dumb thing we'd done, or prod our courage up. So I can't claim I paid much attention to what they were saying.

Now, I wasn't aiming to get drunk that night. Some Fridays, I had just that in mind, but not that night. Maybe it was because Turp was there. But I kept on sipping every time after I looked at him. He was sitting real quiet over in a corner, not at all what I'd expected. He'd been so hellfire ready to come that I counted on him acting the fool just because he could be there drinking with us. But he didn't. For the better part of an hour he didn't do a durn thing except stay in his corner and sip shine. Actually, he was sipping right steady and I guess his shine was warming him up like my whiskey was doing me, cause pretty soon he shucked his coat and then a few minutes later he unbuttoned the cuff buttons on his checkered shirt and rolled the sleeves up.

"Sure am glad you guys let me join you," he said, his voice squeaking a little like he hadn't used it in a long time and it had gone rusty.

"Welcome," J.D. said.

Lonnie waggled his harmonica at him and grinned big. Easy to see that Lonnie was starting to enjoy his evening.

Seeing as how I was the one that, in a way, had asked him to come, I probably should have said at least a word or two, made him feel welcome. Only, deep down inside, every time I looked at his long, narrow face I felt guilty. And when a man feels guilty for a time it's easy for that guilt to turn into hate. So I just nodded and tried not to think about Turp's wife.

"Sure is nice of you all," Turp said. "I mean real nice, cause I ain't been nowhere with a bunch of fellows in a long time. 'Cept for work, a course." He sniffed a little like he was getting teared up. "Gets sort of lonesome, you know, just a going home every day after the shift."

"Yeah," Lonnie said, rocking forward as he spoke, "but you got a wife to go home to. According to what I hear, she's a real looker."

Turp pulled a handkerchief out of his back pocket and snorted into it. "Yeah, Marta's pretty alright, but she ain't quite right."

"What you mean, she's ain't right?"

"She's not all there. Even her daddy admits that."

"You mean to say your wife is a brick shy of a load?"

Turp looked down at the floor for what seemed like a long time. It got real quiet in that old cabin. Then he looked up and said, "That's exactly what I mean." Turp took another slug of shine. A big one. "Why she don't think about nothing except one thing."

Somehow I knew what Turp was a-fixing to say and I sure as hell hoped he would just shut up. But I guess some folks just got to tell all they know, or at least what they think. Or maybe it was really a confession. From conversations I'd overheard in the mine, I knew Turp went to church some, and when he went, he went to the old Hardshell Baptist Church down on Big Mud Lick. Even though I wasn't a church goer, I knew the Baptists, especially the Hardshell variety, was big on confession.

Lonnie had to egg him on, of course. That was just his way. He was a good guy, give you the shirt right off his back, but he did love to stir the pot. "And what that's one thing she keeps a thinking on, Turp?" he said, and then he snickered like a schoolboy.

For a minute I thought Turp wasn't going to answer. His face just got all red and he swole up some like a bullfrog, but then he blurted out, "Oh you know, Lonnie, you know, damn it to hell, you know how women is," and then he drug his old handkerchief around and buried his face in it. "And I can't satisfy her," he mumbled through the handkerchief, "don't think no man could." I could see Turp's shoulders shaking and I wished he'd just drink himself to sleep and then sleep for a long time.

Naturally, Lonnie and J.D. both burst out laughing and started cracking jokes.

Inside my mind it was like a nest of snakes starting to crawl on the first warm day in April. I kept thinking about Marta and old Asa and the verses out of the Bible and what God would want me to do. Only God was way too high a mark for me to ever reach, so I just tried to figure out what Mr. Whitman would do about the situation. But all that thinking and trying to see a way clear made my head ache and I took a long swallow to ease the aching.

Lonnie and J.D. had got to playing high card and was matching for pennies from a deck J.D. carried. Turp had unbuttoned all the buttons on his shirt so that you could see his chest. He'd also starting singing to himself, real low so that all you could tell was that he was singing. I had to take a leak, so I buttoned my coat up good and walked on outside. The wind was rising again and was sharp enough to take your breath. I could hear it whining off in the pines and rattling loose boards on one end of the old cabin. The air felt like ice and smelled like snow.

Underbrush and scrub cedars and sassafras had grown up close to the house since the old man had died and I didn't have to wander far. I stepped behind a clump of sumac and laurel and did my business. When I'd finished, I stood there for some time, just listening to something small and alive rustling in the brush pile on down the slope and the hooting of an owl deeper off in the timber and night falling all around.

From far down the hill, I could hear the sound of moving water. Horse Blood Branch ran along the bottom of a steep ravine. Usually it was a shallow stream, lined with dark rocks, running clear and cold. When the spring rains came, it was prone to flooding. It had got its name years ago, back when the county was just being settled, and some poor farmer's horses got spooked and ran off the edge of the cliff and fell to the rocks below. According to the legend, their blood had turned the water of the creek red. I didn't disbelieve that story, Horse Blood Branch ran through some of the rockiest, most rugged land I knew.

I looked up at the sky, hoping to see the moon, or even a star. But all I could see was the dark underbelly of the clouds. The wind was cold enough and blowing hard enough to cut right on through my coat. Felt like that wind was tattooing me with an icicle. I heard the door to the old cabin creak open and I turned and saw a figure step out in the bar of light.

At first, I figured it was Turp, but as the man drew closer I could see it was J.D. walking across the dead grass. I stepped on out of the undergrowth and J.D. shifted his angle and came toward me, shivering a little.

"Damn," he said, "colder than a witch's titty out here."

"Gets your attention, for sure."

"What the hell you doing out here, Eddie? Playing with your horndog self?"

"Naw, just getting some air."

"Well, what you'd best be getting is back inside."

"Why?"

"Why? 'Cause that nut Turp you begged to let come has done gone loco."

"What do you mean, gone loco?"

"I mean the weirdo is a taking off all his clothes. Done got his shirt and shoes and britches off and now he's down to his shorts and Lonnie's a trying to keep them on the durn idiot."

"Quit fooling, J.D."

"I ain't fooling. Turp's gone crazy. Maybe it's the shine, I don't know. But what I do know is that he is trying to take all his clothes off and laughing and crying at the same time."

"Damn," I said, and started for the cabin, cursing Turp under my breath and feeling the night closing in around me. J.D. stumbled once and banged against me and I staggered but stayed upright. Halfway to the cabin, I could hear someone screaming. Before I opened the door I paused and had a quick bracer. As I was putting the bottle back in my coat, I could hear J.D.'s bottle gurgling.

It was just like J.D. had said. Turp was down to his underwear and Lonnie had him trapped in a corner. Turp's face was flushed and his hair was wild. His eyes looked wet.

"Keep your damn drawers on," Lonnie said.

"But I've got to show you," Turp said.

"Show me what?"

"My embarrassment."

"What the hell you talking about? Your wiener?"

"Get away from me, I've got to show you." Without warning, Turp lunged left. Lonnie moved with him, but his feet got tangled and he stumbled into the wall. Turp cut back right and ran across the room to the far corner. I started to go after him, but J.D. grabbed my arm.

"He's getting himself all worked up. Some kind of a fit. Must be bad shine he's been drinking. Maybe we better let him alone."

"Alright," I said, and, even though I didn't want to, I stood there looking at Turp.

In seconds, he had his underwear off. He flung it on the floor and pointed at his privates. He was swaying a little, like he was a white pine in a stout breeze, but it was still easy to see what he was talking about. His penis was just a stub. Looked like it belonged on a little boy. Not in ten lifetimes would I have shown that. I wasn't hung like a horse myself, but his little skinny stub was pitiful. Why in the name of all that was holy would he volunteer to show that? I looked away.

"I'll be damned," J.D. said.

"Shit," Lonnie said and sat down against the wall.

All I wanted to do was get out of there, but it was cold and dark and if I wasn't half drunk I was well on my way. Waiting for daylight seemed to be the only option.

"Don't it get bigger when you get a hard-on?" J.D. asked.

In between sobs Turp choked out "No." I glanced at J.D. and he just shook his head. "What can you say?" he muttered and walked back to his corner.

He was right. Wasn't anything to say or do, except maybe take another drink. So I did. I'd planned to save back about half the pint, but now I just wanted to drink the night out of my mind.

I wandered over to a vacant corner and sat down and started sipping steady. Lots of Friday nights Lonnie would bring potatoes from his garden and we'd build a fire and roast them in the ashes. Tonight, nobody had been paying attention and the fire had burned down almost to embers and if Lonnie had brought potatoes he hadn't said anything about them. My sandwiches weren't enough to hold me comfortably till daylight and I wished I had something to nibble on. Since I didn't, I just sipped on whiskey and thought about poor Turp and Marta and how I figured in to that equation. Algebra had always been beyond me.

After a while, Turp quit crying and I got up and crossed the room and picked up his coat where he'd slung it and walked over to his corner. He was lying down now, on his side, sniffing and mumbling something I couldn't make out. Somehow, he'd hung on to his shine and I could see he only had a couple of inches left. That stuff can flat out knock your socks off, so it wasn't any wonder he'd gone a little nuts.

I figured on taking the jar of shine away from him, but he had a death grip on it, so I just spread his coat out over him the best I could. As I turned to go, he spoke. "Eddie?"

"What?"

"I'm sorry."

"Don't worry," I said. "Things will look better in the daylight."

"No they won't. They never do. You know I can't even get really hard. I ain't made right."

"Ah, come on, Turp, It's not that bad. Sometimes you just have to deal with things."

"But I can't. Not this."

"Oh, grow up." He was crying again. I can't stand to see men cry and he was crying.

"Help me, Eddie, please help me."

Before I could think of what to say, Turp grabbed hold of my right ankle. I tried to shake his hand off but his fingers gripped like a vice. "Let go, damn you." I tried to jerk away, but his grip was too strong. Never could stand having my feet bound. I wanted to scream. Instead, I bent down and hit him in the face. Guess I hit him pretty hard. Anyway, my knuckles hurt afterwards.

I only hit him the one time, but that was enough for him to let go. In a way, I felt bad about hitting him, but I couldn't see any other solution.

"You hate me," he sobbed.

What I should have said was "No, I don't," but something wouldn't let me even open my mouth. Just stood there staring down at Turp. Even in the poor light from the fire, I could see tears on his face. Right then maybe I did hate him. Hate's a sin. Even a heathen like me knew that. But he was such a crybaby and a whiner. Reckon, at least for a few hours, I truly did hate him.

"Nobody likes me. Even Marta don't like me. She laughs at me. She takes my money and laughs at me."

Maybe there were some words I should have said that would have made him feel better. If there were I couldn't think of them, not then. Never was much good in an argument. It's not that I'm stupid, more like I get mad and can only think of things a long time after.

No, I didn't know what to say. How the hell was a man supposed to respond to a man who wasn't really quite a man? It crossed my mind to ask him how he and Marta did things, but I didn't. Just didn't say anything. Only stood there trying not to judge. That was one of the Sunday School lessons I did remember, "Judge not, lest ye be judged." But, like a whole lot of the Bible, while it sure sounded good it was damn hard to do.

"I'm so sorry," he said.

"What's done is done, so don't apologize." My anger was starting to cool and now all I wanted was to get away from him. Felt guilty about that, but that's the way I am.

"Try and get some sleep," I said. Then, even though it was hard for me, I bent down and patted him on the shoulder. I could tell that he wanted to talk about things, but I just didn't see how I could. So I left him there, mumbling to himself, sniffing. Maybe he'll pass out soon, I told myself.

Nobody had much to say the rest of the night. After Turp's exhibition what was there to talk about. On my way back to my corner, I poked at the embers and chucked a small log on the flames. Guess everybody had been anxious to get to drinking cause that was the next to last log. I hoped one of the others would get cold enough to go out and bring in some wood from the pile we'd cut and stacked at the corner of the house back in the summer. Suppose we could have played some poker, but last time that game cost me over three dollars. Tonight I'd have given twenty to have never even come.

It had been a long week and with enough whiskey I began to get sleepy. I told myself I'd stay awake and keep an eye on Turp. He was in bad shape. He wouldn't stay down and he'd finished off the shine and was bumming drinks off of the rest of us. He wouldn't put his clothes back on, but J.D. and Lonnie had at least talked him into putting his jacket on. Now and then he would sit down, but the next minute he'd be up staggering around the room crying and carrying on, crying out for Marta. For a while he got on a talking jag and it sounded like he was trying to apologize to somebody, maybe his grandpa. Gradually, he began to wind down and he settled down in a corner with his back against the wall and started singing softly. He didn't have a bad voice, but I didn't know the song. Sounded like an old ballad, a slow and mournful one. Somewhere in the night I drifted off to sleep.

***

Deep in the night I came awake mumbling to myself. If I had been dreaming the dream had disappeared. I'd never woke up talking to myself before. I was saying something about being my brother's keeper. Vaguely, I could recall a preacher talking about that when I was a kid. Remember that because I had so many brothers I couldn't imagine how I could take care of all of them.

The fire had died down and the room was cold. J.D. was huddled up in one corner and Lonnie was stretched out on his stomach directly in front of the fire. He was snoring.

Shivering, I got up, stepped over Lonnie, and poked around in the embers. I put the last log on the fire. It was good-sized. I hoped it would burn till morning. Then I rubbed my hands together and did a few knee bends and arm swings and tried to warm up. The arm swings weren't such a good idea. I was still a little blitzed and the movement made me about half dizzy.

When the room grew still, I meandered over and peered out the window. The sky was smoothed over and gray. Snowflakes were drifting in the wind. Just looking at the falling snow made me colder.

Stray thoughts started bumping together in the back of my mind. Something didn't seem quite right. Whiskey still had a grip on my brain and it took a little while to figure out what was off kilter.

Turp wasn't in the room.

Just to make sure, I looked around the room twice. In spite of the cold I wasn't quite awake and I had a nice start on a real old-fashioned hangover. What I really wanted to do was curl up next to the fire and go to sleep, but Turp was out in the cold somewhere and I felt at least partially responsible. I took a deep breath and started walking. Maybe I should have woke Lonnie and J.D. up, but at that moment all I could think of was Turp running around in the dark wearing only his coat and the snow sure enough falling. Just thinking about it made my blood ice.

7

AT DAYLIGHT I FOUND HIM.

Actually, I saw his body.

I'd worked my way all around the perimeter of the cabin and then through the underbrush that grew close to what had been the yard. Snow fell in squalls and then the wind died and I could hear the water far below and, once, the whistle of the coal train headed toward Manchester from Driftwood #2. I called out Turp's name, but only my echo came back from the hillside.

Twice I went back inside to warm up. The other two slept as innocent as a couple of old hound dogs. The second time I noticed that Lonnie had an extra half-pint and there was a swig left in one of the bottles. I helped myself. Needed all the anti-freeze I could get.

When I went back out the second time the eastern sky rim had turned pale blue. Trees loomed up like giant soldiers and I could hear birds twittering. When my eyes had adjusted, I could make out the start of a path that snaked off down the hill toward the heavy timber. Beyond the heavy timber was a patch of rocky ground, with brambles and kudzu growing up between the rocks. Go far enough and the land came to an abrupt end. One step a man was on solid rock. The next and his foot pushed through air. It was a helluva long way to the bottom of Horse Blood Branch.

Picking my way carefully, I eased down the slope. A frosting of snow coated the tree branches and the bare ground. Deep in a pine thicket, I could hear my own breathing. My head was pounding and my body was quivering with the cold, but I pushed on.

I didn't call his name now. The air had gone lighter the way it does right before daylight. You think you can see then, but pre-dawn light is tricky. I'd been pushing down right steady for about ten minutes and knew I had to be getting close to the edge of the cliff. I didn't trust the light, or the footing, or my nerves, so I eased down, clinging to tree branches, watching where I placed my feet.

Even going so slow, land's end slipped up on me. A jaybird had started screeching in a stand of oaks and I was half-looking at him, thinking maybe Turp was close by and spooking him and I damned near walked into the nothingness.

Instinct, I guess, made me turn and when I did all I could see was air. My legs buckled and I went down on some rocks. In all my life I'd never been so glad to scrape my knees.

When I got my breath back, I worked up nerve and, with a good grip on solid rock, I leaned over the edge and looked down.

Never had flown in an airplane, but I figured looking down from that cliff must be something like looking out of the windows of a plane. At first all I could see was light reflecting off water and then I could make out boulders. In that early light they looked white. Then I could see something dark splayed out on one of those white boulders. Just from the shape of it I knew.

Part of me wanted to cry and another part wanted

to scream. It was all I could do to keep from gagging on my own vomit. All that passed in a moment and then the sun was cresting the ridge line and I could see clear for certain. If I'd been thinking straight I'd a gone back to the cabin and stretched out in front of what was left of the fire and told the world I'd never been out of that cabin except for the once to piss. But seeing something like that don't truly allow a man to think straight. For a spell, I just sat on a rock and thought about the morning being born again and Turp deader than a hammer down on Horse Blood Branch and what I needed to do. After I got things inside my mind untangled some, I got up and started back for the cabin.

8

TOOK ME AND J.D. all morning to haul Turp's body out of that ravine. Lonnie had driven to town to notify the Sheriff. First, though, he'd hauled me and J.D. around to the mouth of the creek. We'd hiked back in a good mile before we saw Turp sprawled out like he was sleeping off a bad night. Scrambling over the rocks to reach him, I thought to myself that at least he won't have any more bad nights, nor bad days.

You wouldn't think a dead man would be hard to handle, but you'd be wrong. All dead weight and starting to stiffen, he didn't smell so good and the ground was steep and rocky and every rock seemed sharp-edged. It was like some giant had gone through that territory hundreds of years ago and sharpened every rock with his whetstone just for the pure devilment of it. By the time we'd carried, and drug, Turp's body out to the old Jackson Road, I was sweating and J.D. was cussing under his breath.

"Now what?" he asked.

Turp's body was just lying by the side of the road like some dog that had been hit by a car and crawled off the highway to die. "All I know to do is wait for the sheriff or Lonnie to show up." The sky was still gray and what little light filtered through had no real heat.

"For a dead man he sure was heavy."

"Guess most people are heavy dead, or alive."

"Damn, that wind is cold and I've got a hangover that would kill a full grown buffalo. Sure wish somebody would come along," J.D. said. He looked down at Turp. "Wish we could cover him up. Hate the way his eyes keep staring at us like he thinks we killed him."

I wanted to tell J.D. to shut the hell up. Just being near Turp gave me the creeps. Hadn't cared much for him alive and I sure didn't like him dead. Waiting for Lonnie or the Sheriff to show up seemed like a prison sentence. Even though I felt guilt pinching me for the way things had turned out, having to stay with the body while the wind iced his bones and mine seemed too much.

I could hear birds in the trees across the road. Cardinals. Red arrows flickering from tree to tree. There must have been nine or ten. They looked like smears of blood among the evergreens.

Ice pellets whirled in the wind now and stung my face. For the first time I could remember, I wished I was down in the hole working on a Saturday. The whistle was blowing over at the old tipple. Second shift must be coming on, or maybe the unit train was loading. My head hurt. I kept sneaking looks at Turp like his body was a magnet. My stomach had been churning all morning and every time I looked at him I felt sicker. Up on the hill there was a shotgun blast. My left eye twitched. I knew I was going to throw up. Without looking careful, I crossed the road and puked my guts out in the ditch. Tears filled my eyes like I was crying. Guess I owed old Turp a few tears, but then my stomach rolled again and I puked some more.

***

Halfway to dark Lonnie rolled up, tires loud on the gravel. J.D. had dozed off. He sat up blinking like an owl will when a sudden light shines in his eyes. "About damn time," he said.

Before we could get up from the bank Lonnie was getting out of the car. He walked around the front and leaned over and looked down at the body. About an hour ago, it had started to snow again, just light stuff, flurries really, and J.D. and I had crawled back on the bank under a big old white pine. We'd left Turp where he lay and now I could see snow in his hair and on his face. Snow was even in his eyes. Seeing that snow starting to cover him like that made me sick again, but I looked away real quick and choked it down.

"Where's the sheriff?"

"Gone clear to Laughton. Somebody stole all of Judge Taylor's cattle and a hundred and forty-seven dollars cash money. Ben Prewitt said the judge was pissed. Claimed Taylor said he'd hang the man what done it."

"Ain't nobody coming?"

"Not before tomorrow anyway. I told Ben Prewitt everything. He said he'd tell the sheriff. What about Jerry Conley? Ain't he still coroner?"

Lonnie shook his head. "That fool wrecked his ambulance last week going to Hazard. Broke both legs and is still in the hospital. Be there another week, they say."

"Well, hell," J.D. said, "what are we going to do? Can't stay here all night. We'd freeze to death. Plus, my old lady's probably been looking for me for hours. If I don't show up soon she's liable to shoot me when I come in the door."

Lonnie nodded at Turp. "Can't leave him here, that's for dang sure."

"Load his dead ass in the trunk," J.D. said. "I ain't going to freeze my ass off for no corpse. Not for nobody, and that includes Turp Lawson, even if I did work alongside the man."

The snow was coming down harder now. The wind was driving it. I could feel my entire body shivering. Couldn't remember being so cold. It was like the wind had gotten into my bones. Guess somebody will have to tell his wife." I said.

J.D. had bent down and grabbed Turp by both ankles. He looked up and grinned at me. "Buddy, that would be you, 'cause you're the one what asked him to come."

"I never asked him," I said.

"Close enough," J.D. said.

"Right," said Lonnie. "That job is purely yours, Fast Eddie. Now grab an arm and let's get him in the trunk afore we all freeze to death."

"God damn," I said under my breath and bent over. Turp's arm felt like cold steel. He was cold and stiff and heavy and I wanted to vomit again.

***

"Where we going?" J.D. asked. He was sitting up front with Lonnie and I was in back, shivering with the cold. Lonnie's heater didn't work except two ways— poorly and intermittently. I'd been staring out the window. The glass was splattered with mud and froze-on leaves and it was hard to see much, but now and then I saw a few snowflakes, falling real slow and easy and swirling in the wind. Paul D. Hoskins, my cousin, had told me when I was just a kid that snowflakes were the eyes of dead angels falling from heaven. After that, I'd not cared for snow ice cream.

"Hell if I know," Lonnie said, "but we've got to get shed of this body afore long. I don't aim to drive old Turp back to my place."

"Guess we ought to take him into town." J.D. said. "Maybe Doc McKee will know what to do with the corpse."

"Doc McKee's gone to Ohio for the weekend. Heard him tell the Powers boys down at the drug store last Saturday that he was aiming to go visit his sister up to Portsmouth." Lonnie twisted his neck and glanced back for a second. "What about it, Fast Eddie, where do think we ought to go?"

I'd been thinking on that and answered right back. "Maybe we ought to go see Mr. Whitman."

"Now why the hell didn't I think of that?" Lonnie said. "Mr. Whitman knows just about everything that goes on in this county. He'll know what to do. Agreed?" J.D. nodded but I didn't say anything because it had been my idea to begin with. About two miles down the road Lonnie cut the wheel and we swung left and hit the old Clintonville Road. Mr. Whitman lived a short piece off that road up on Folly Mountain.

Before we got to the turnoff J.D. had passed out and if I'd been warmer guess I'd done the same. But it seemed like a real hard chill had settled all the way down in my bones and I just couldn't get warm. Uncle Seth, my mother's brother, had gone to Florida back in the Depression looking for work in the orange groves and the last we heard from him he'd saved back enough to start up a fishing camp. That had been several years ago, but, riding in that cold car looking out the window at the snow flurrying down, I sure wished I was down at that camp, and I'm not a man who's crazy for fishing.

Mr. Whitman was standing out in his yard with a splitting maul in one hand and a stack of split logs off to one side. His old border collie was lying at his feet. Guess the dog had been snoozing cause when we drove up he eased up, barked a couple of times and gave us an evil eye. For as long as I could remember that dog had gone most places with Mr. Whitman. Many's the day I'd seen him up at the mine, either sitting in the cab of Mr. Whitman's truck or wandering around behind the boss as he talked with one of his foremen or maybe some miner he was asking after. That got me to wondering how long I'd worked for the man. Never really kept track, but it must be getting on for ten years.

Lonnie's car screeched to a stop at a turnaround. For six months he'd been going to get some brake work done. We all got out of the car and trudged up the graveled slope. Mr. Whitman didn't seem particularly surprised to see us. Probably because lots of Saturday morning a miner or two who'd spent all his payday Friday night on whiskey or woman, or lost it at Bud Renfro's poker game, would show up needing a loan to tide him over. All three of us were still hung over to one degree or another and we hadn't shaved or cleaned up or even changed clothes. As we crossed the yard, I wondered what he was thinking. Whatever it was he didn't show it, just said "Hello, men," like it was another day at the mines.

I hung back and saw Lonnie look at J.D. and J.D. nod his head straight at Lonnie and next I heard Lonnie sigh real loud. We all came to a stop about the same exact time, just like we were in the army and J.D. and I both looked at Lonnie. His eyes looked like a wild animal, say a fox, that had got a paw caught in a steel trap. For a second he stared at us, then he turned and faced Mr. Whitman.

Lonnie licked his lips and took a deep breath. I could hear a cardinal calling out down along a line of barbed wire Mr. Whitman had strung to keep his beef cattle out of his wife's flower bed. According to the tales he told now and again, his wife was a woman who took great pride in her iris and hydrangeas.

"Cold one, ain't it?" Lonnie finally spit out.

Mr. Whitman nodded. He was wearing a leather cap with the ear flaps turned up and I could see his white hair. The man had a real head of hair, all of it white as snow. Heard he gone completely white haired before he turned thirty. But I didn't know him then. He had a hard-boned face. Not a mean one, mind you, but you could see at a glance that he was a man you didn't want to cross.

"Wind is a bit sharp," he allowed.

Lonnie nodded and grinned and rubbed the steel toe of one boot across the grass. It was clear as Sunday morning that he was having a hard time coming to the point. The cardinal flew just then and I saw him out of the corner of one eye, winging it for a blue spruce smack in the middle of Mr. Whitman's front yard.

Mr. Whitman leaned his maul against a stump and raked his eyes across us. "What can I do for you boys?"

I looked at the others. J.D.'s head was hanging down and Lonnie just had a goofy grin on his face. "Well," I said, because somebody had to say something, "we got something in the trunk we need to show you, Mr. Whitman."

Maybe my voice sounded strange cause he gave me a funny look. Then he said, "All right," and started walking toward the car. Lonnie hustled up then and got in front and popped the trunk.

For what seemed like a long time, but I don't guess was more than a few seconds, Mr. Whitman just stood there looking at the corpse in the trunk of Lonnie's old car. Turp wasn't a real pretty sight. The fall must have broken his cheekbones on one side, cause his face was caved in there. Dried blood was streaked all over and there were scratches and dirt on his face, too. Guess those scratches were where J.D. and I hadn't handled him strictly gentle like getting him out of that creek bottom.

Nobody said a word. We were all looking at Turp, or what was left of him. The day had gone real quiet. I could hear the wind in the tops of the trees and the cattle far off in the field and the old dog scratching himself. I wondered what the boss was thinking. In the end all he said was, "What happened?"

He said it real calm like and I guess we were all expecting him to cuss or shout or carry on some way because we just stood there like dumb animals. Finally, Lonnie said, "Well, Mr. Whitman, we was all doing a little drinking last night over at the cabin, you know, and it got kind of late and I suppose the three of us dozed off and Turp, well we thought he was asleep, too, but he must have woke up and wandered off and somehow the durn fool fell off the cliff and smashed up on the rocks along Horse Blood Branch."

"That's right, Mr. Whitman," J.D. said, "and me and Eddie, well, we hauled him out to the road and Lonnie went to report to the sheriff. Only he's out of town and so is Doc McKee. So we figured we ought to report it to somebody official like. And, seeing as how Turp worked for you, why we drove on down here."

Mr. Whitman turned then and looked each of us square in the eyeballs. Right then the wind blew extra cold and I could feel my whole body shivering like I had the flu.

"Well," he said, finally, "guess we're going to have to see about getting him buried. Now, if I remember straight, Turp's mom and dad have both passed."

"That's right, Mr. Whitman," Lonnie said. "His dad got killed timbering six, seven years ago and his mother's heart give out not long after that."

"Turp have any brothers or sisters?"

"No, sir."

"What about other kin?"

"None I know of," Lonnie said. "That branch of the Lawson clan just sort of petered out. Reckon two of his dad's brothers, Turp's uncles, got killed in the war. D-Day, if I heard right."

J.D. shook his head.

"He had a wife," I said.

Mr. Whitman looked directly at me. "You know her?"

"I've met her."

"What's her name?"

"Marta. She's a blonde girl, maybe not quite right in the head, if you know what I mean."

"I'd heard something about that. Her daddy runs a grocery store in town, I believe."

"That's right."

"Pretty girl, but not all there?"

I nodded.

"That's what I figured. Oh well, so be it." Mr. Whitman frowned and then he looked up toward his house and then out over the field where his cattle were. Two of them were grazing at the top of the slope. They were fat and black. Seeing them reminded me that it had been a long time since I'd eaten. Hard to believe, but I was sort of hungry.

We all waited on Mr. Whitman to speak. He took his time. Studying on how to plan it all out, I suppose. Finally, he nodded like he come to agreement with himself.

"Alright, here's what we'll do. Lonnie, you and J.D. take Turp over to your house and get him cleaned up best you can. Then, drive over to Mote Wilson's. Mote will have a casket handy. Always keeps a couple in the back. Pick one out, a plain pine will do fine, and tell him I'll settle with him later. Then get Turp over to the little church at the Goshen Junction. I've heard him tell he goes to church there some.

"Eddie, you'll have to let his wife know and tell her what we're doing. I know her family, and none of their kids had sense to come in out of the rain. The old man is pretty sharp, but all he ever cared for was making money and the mother never was the brightest bulb in the pack. Doug Bowling is her brother. Years ago he worked for me. Wrecked one of my best trucks, acting silly. Had to let him go. Wonder what ever happened to him?"

Mr. Whitman fell silent then and I guess he was looking back over the years. I was just so pure tired that I'd started to doze off when he cleared his throat.

"We'll want some nice clothes to bury him in. Mine would be way too big. How about you J.D., you got an old suit coat?"

"No sir, Mr. Whitman, I sure don't."

Right then I recalled an old suit jacket and some trousers I had. The suit was patched on both elbows and the pants was unraveling at the bottom of the legs, but that wouldn't matter none, him being in a casket.

"Guess I've got a coat and trousers that would work," I said.

"Good deal," Mr. Whitman said. "I'll drive you over to Turp's place and you can tell his widow and then go get the suit. I'll run into town and talk to my lawyer, who's the county attorney, then I'll pick you back up at the mine. Then we'll go over to the church."

He paused and turned and looked at J.D. and Lonnie. "You boys get him cleaned up real nice and we'll see you at the church. Now, I'd better go tell the wife and get my billfold." He looked at me and his eyes could have been stones. "You wait here."

"Sure," I said, and he turned and walked on up the slope toward his house. I stood there in the yard and watched Lonnie and J.D. walk back down the slope and get in the car. After a minute they drove off. The wind was blowing hard now and I stood there in the yard shivering and wishing Mr. Whitman would hurry. Then I wished that I'd never laid eyes on Turp or his goofy wife. Right then that hillside seemed about the most lonely spot I'd ever been.

***

After a few minutes Mr. Whitman came out wearing a nice topcoat and a stylish hat. He was carrying a cup in each hand. "Want some coffee?"

"Sure," I said, "and thanks."

"We'll drink as we go. Lots to do today."

Cradling the cup, savoring its warmth, I walked around to the passenger side of Mr. Whitman's truck and climbed in. He got in behind the wheel and handed me his cup. I held both cups while he turned the pickup in the yard and maneuvered down the drive. Once we were out on the road, I handed him his cup and took a sip from mine. I needed coffee bad.

"I'm still not clear on what happened last night, Eddie. Can you fill me in?"

I looked at him then. But he was staring straight down the road and I couldn't read him at all. I took another hit off my coffee while I thought.

"Happened about like we told you back at the house, Mr. Whitman. Since we'd all been drinking, and don't guess any of us could swear in court, but Turp had to have wandered off in the night and fell off the cliff. I mean he was pretty liquored up, Mr. Whitman."

"What was he drinking?"

"Some shine he got off the Miller boy down on Croley Bend."

"Something wrong with the shine?"

I shrugged. "Couldn't say, Mr. Whitman. Didn't drink any of his stuff. None of us did. We were all drinking out of our own bottle."

Mr. Whitman took a quick sip of coffee and glanced at me. He had one hand on the wheel. "Didn't know Turp Lawson hung out with you and J.D. and Lonnie."

"Last night was the first time he ever went drinking with us. Been after me to let him come for some time, but last night was the first."

"Did he seem alright? I mean did he act like something was bothering him?"

There didn't seem to be an easy way to answer that

question. I needed a few seconds to think, so I looked out the window. The remnants of a cornfield stood off the road on my side. The stalks were dead and brown and as I watched a flock of small dark birds rose from the field and swirled above like a strange feathered whirlwind.

"Most of the time he was alright, I guess, but he kept carrying on about personal stuff and then, well, I hate to tell you Mr. Whitman, but he started taking off his clothes, hollering about how small he was. Down there, I mean." I hated to talk about Turp, especially his inadequacies. Embarrassing as hell to talk about another man's pecker. "His privates, see."

"Turp must have been plastered."

"Been hitting it pretty hard."

"And did he?"

"Did he what?"

"Take off his clothes."

"We tried to stop him, Mr. Whitman, but he just kept drinking and carrying on and finally he got them all off." I could feel the heat running up the side of my neck and couldn't make myself look at Mr. Whitman. My coffee was going cold, so I tipped the cup up and drank the rest.

"And was he? Small, like he said?"

"Yeah, kind of. I mean not that I really looked, but he was carrying on so it was hard not to notice." I looked at Mr. Whitman then. Out of the corners of my eyes so he wouldn't know about it. The man made me nervous. He seemed to know just about everything without me telling him. His eyes were staring straight ahead and his face was closed up. I wondered what he was thinking. I sure hoped he couldn't read minds.

"And you don't know what was making him act that

way, Eddie?"

Right off I could see that question was full of sharp points. Kind of like picking blackberries. No matter how I answered one of those thorns was going to stick me. Plus my mind was still full of cobwebs and my brain was pounding. A cup of coffee had helped, but a gallon would have been better. Straight shot of whiskey would have been the best medicine.

Lying to Mr. Whitman wasn't a good idea, and I really didn't want to anyway. But I couldn't see how telling everything I knew would help anybody. So I finally told a truth, but not, like they say in court, the whole truth and nothing but the truth, so help you God. Now, I didn't know about God. He might forgive a man, if you can believe the Bible. But Mr. Whitman wasn't a man who put up with liars. That I knew for a certain fact.

"Mr. Whitman, it's real hard to say for sure what was on that man's mind. He was drunk and acting crazy. Even cried some. Remember he did keep saying that nobody loved him and, even though he never did give what you'd call a lot of details, he gave the impression that he and his wife had maybe been fighting."

I kept expecting Mr. Whitman to ask me more questions, but all he said was, "I see."

For a while I worried about what he saw, or thought he saw. Then for a bit we went through some switchbacks and then we were rolling along the spine of the ridge and I could see the valley below. It was so far away that the houses looked like doll furniture and once we hit the gravel on the outside shoulder and I thought about Turp falling and some of the coffee came back up and I had to choke it down and it burned in my throat and I thought I was going to be sick. But when we hit the crest and the road turned back toward the center of the bluff I was alright. Only my head was pounding like some troll had crawled inside there with a ball peen hammer and was swinging it steady. I was glad when we got to the head of the holler and Mr. Whitman pulled over, even if I did dread what I had to do next.

9

TOOK ME LONGER THAN I figured to find my old sports coat and when I got it out in the light I could see that the sleeves below the elbows were shiny. And the pants weren't strictly clean, what with a stain on one of the legs. But the spot was down low and I figured people wouldn't notice that. After folding them the best I could, I put them in a paper sack.

Before I started cleaning myself up, I fed and watered Trips and opened up a can of soup I'd forgotten about. Actually, it was more of a stew. Hadn't realized how hungry I was. Old Trips was sure glad to see me, too. I scratched him behind the ears and then he stretched out and I rubbed his belly with the toe of my boot. My brain still felt like it was cracking open, so I dry swallowed a couple of packets of Goody's headache powders.

Then I fired up the stove and put a pan of water on. While the water was heating, I pulled out the clothes I wanted to wear. Then I washed up, scrubbing real good, using a bar of soap I found behind some Mason jars in the pantry. Expect Mom put it there; toward the end she got sorta absentminded.

By the time I was clean and dressed I was finally good and warm, and, what with my belly full, I was getting sleepy. After all, I'd been through one hell of a rough twenty-four hours. Never had been much for taking naps, but I figured it wouldn't hurt to lie down for a few minutes and rest my eyes. Scrubbing the dirt off made me feel rather virtuous somehow and the old house had gone quiet and my eyelids felt like somebody had poured sand on them. It felt strange knowing that a dead man would soon be wearing your clothes, especially since I'd gone to bed with his wife, but I closed my eyes and tried to make my mind still, like the stillness that comes over the surface of a pond on a windless day.

When I woke up, the day had gone on and grown old without me. No dreams, but there was a nasty taste in my mouth and a nagging feeling at the base of my brain that I'd missed something important.

My legs were stiff and trying to cramp up and I rolled off the old horsehair couch that had been my great-grandmother's and stumbled over to the window, swearing with every step that I'd never drink again, knowing full well I would.

The sun had already slipped behind the hills and the light was fading. There was a blue cast to the air that evening and I wondered if that was a sign, like a blue moon meant that somebody close was going to die. Wasn't any time to think about that though, I'd slept too long and should have been at the mine already. Grabbing the bag with the clothes, I hurried out the door. Trips tried to follow, but I yelled at him and chucked a rock close enough to send him hightailing it for the house. A dog underfoot was one more thing I didn't need this day.

Shadows were deep and blue and covering the road by the time I passed Asa's place. He wasn't out on the porch, but I waved in case he was peering out the window. When I got to the good road I started running. Not hard like a bear was after me, but a good steady pace that covered the ground. Back in school I'd been one of the best runners in my class. In those days I could have run all the way to Turp's place without straining, but school had been years ago and booze and smokes aren't the best training tools and I had to walk in places.

Hard dusk covered the earth by the time I sighted Turp's place. It was one of those places you came on real sudden. One minute you were moving through a thicket of young poplars and then, without a hint of warning, you popped out into a clearing and there stood his house at the other edge of the clearing.

Lights burned inside and spilled out into the yard and I slowed to a walk, partly to catch my breath and partly to give me a little time to think what I needed to say. Sure wasn't looking forward to seeing Marta. At best, it was going to be embarrassing. I'd have to choose my words carefully.

Guess she saw me crossing the open ground. Maybe she was at the window looking for Turp. I figured he'd never been gone this long before. Anyway, before I could knock she was jerking the door open. While I was trying to start talking she grabbed one arm and tugged me inside. I sort of tucked the sack behind my back. I wasn't ready to show her the clothes her husband was going to be buried in.

"Come on in here, you sexy man, you." She lifted her face and kissed me so quick I didn't have time to step away. "Aren't you the bold one coming here to see me while Turp's gone? No wonder they call you Fast Eddie." Then she kissed me again and I let her, though it made my stomach churn. I didn't say a word. Call me a coward at that moment and you wouldn't have been far wrong. But I don't believe I could have told her then what I came to say even if the business end of a knife had been pressing against my throat.

Marta hugged me real tight. Her breasts were mashing against me and her hair was tickling my face. Her tongue was licking along the side of my neck. She had on some sweet smelling perfume and a nice dress and for a second I wondered what it would be like to come home to her every night. Finally, I came back in my right mind and untangled our bodies and stepped back.

Marta put a pouty look on her face. Under other circumstances it might have been cute. "Aren't you happy to see me, Eddie?"

"Sure, but there's something I need to say."

"Oh, you don't have to say anything, you old silly. I know you like me." She stepped forward and before I knew it she had kissed me again, right on the mouth."

"Now listen, Marta," I said, "about Turp."

"Oh, don't worry about Turp. He ain't home yet." She paused and for some reason looked up at the ceiling. Then she looked straight at me. "Never come home at all last night. Knowed he was a-drinkin with you and some of the other men, but I surely thought he'd be to home by now. Turp's not one to miss his dinner."

She patted my cheek in an absentminded way and walked over to the window and stared out across the clearing. Probably I should have told her right then that her husband wasn't ever going to come walking across that yard again. Only I didn't. She turned around and smiled.

"Oh, you're a chancy fellow, Eddie Burke, a-comin here when Turp ain't home. Guess you liked the other afternoon, sure enough. You did, didn't you?"

No way I should have nodded and said "Sure," but that's just what I did. At that moment I didn't think I could handle one more lie, or maybe it was one more sin. All my transgressions were piling up like rocks on my shoulders. Each one of those rocks was heavy, and sharp edged. So, I didn't speak. Only smiled a little because of what I was going to say. Maybe she'd remember the smile and that memory would help a little. Or so I told myself.

Guess Marta took that for encouragement, cause she crossed the floor, almost skipping, and wrapped both arms around my neck. She felt soft and sweet in my arms and I felt like a real bastard as I kissed her.

"What's that you got in that poke behind your back, Eddie baby? Did you bring me a present? Let me see, honey."

I was a real asshole; I know that now and I knew it then. But I suppose I was maybe a little mad at her because if she hadn't come over to my place I'd probably never even kissed her and all this guilt I felt about Turp being dead wouldn't have been hanging around my neck like a logging chain. Anyway, I just handed her the sack and stepped back like she had some sort of disease. Or maybe I just felt unclean.

She was smiling big, like a kid at Christmas, when she opened the sack. Right away her face twisted into this puzzled look. For what seemed like a long time she just stared at the sack. Then, she pulled out the coat and the pants. The bag drifted on down to the floor.

"This here looks like a man's coat and pants," she said. You could hear the puzzlement running through her voice.

"It is," I said.

She looked at me. Her face was all screwed up. "Are they for Turp? Is he going to a party, or something?"

I took another step back and leaned against the wall.

Over Marta's head there was a picture of Jesus hanging beside a mirror. I could see my face in that mirror. Right then, that face made me think of Satan. I sure hoped Marta believed in Jesus.

"They're for Turp, right enough," I said. "Only he isn't going to any party."

"He's not? Then where's he going? Why'd you bring those clothes over here, Eddie?"

I'd never said the first word about him not coming home again, but some way she must have seen something in my face, because her eyes started getting big and her breath began coming in gasps.

"Where's Turp, Eddie, where's my Turp? Answer me, damn you." She was trembling now and fixing to cry. I just shook my head, which only made her mad.

"Quit playing with me, Eddie. I ain't a-liking you no more. Tell me where Turp is. Is he in jail? What has happened?"

I had to swallow a couple of times before I could talk. It was like the words were stuck in my throat, the way little gravels will get stuck in the tread of tires.

"Turp ain't in jail, Marta."

She crossed the floor. Her legs were trembling and she wasn't walking steady. She stumbled into me. Her breath was warm against my face. "Where is he, Eddie? Where's Turp? I know there's something bad wrong by the way you're a looking at me out of the sides of your eyes. You a feared to look straight at me. Things ain't like they were the other day. Know I'm not real smart, but even I can tell that you've changed. Something ain't right. Tell me, Eddie. Tell me."

There had to be better ways to say it, but I couldn't think of any of them. Not then. My face felt all hot and

Snapshot

flushed and I was so nervous I was sweating. Movement caught my eye, and I looked out the window. Just enough light hung in the clearing to make out Mamie Reynolds and Dorothy Hill and a couple of other women I didn't know. They were hurrying across the yard and I figured Lonnie or J.D. or even Mr. Whitman must have told them.

I swallowed again and said, "Turp ain't coming home no more, Marta. There's been a terrible accident, a pure terrible accident."

I'll swear on a stack of Holy Bibles that I aimed to tell her more, that I aimed to tell her the whole truth, or at least what I figured she could handle. Only I hadn't no more got out the word accident than Marta commenced screaming and beating her fists on my chest and those old women must have heard and come running across the yard. For a few minutes it was just pure, unadulterated hell-on-earth, as my Uncle Frank would have said.

Now, I never cared much for Mamie Reynolds or the Widow Hill. They're both a pair of soured up old women who mind everybody else's business, but I freely admit I was glad they were there that day. By the time they pulled Marta off of me she had gone temporarily insane, like they say in court, crying and cursing and speaking in tongues and slobbering all over herself. Blood was dripping down from both my cheeks where she'd scratched me and both my shins were aching. For a woman she sure could kick.

10

GUESS MR. WHITMAN MADE about all of the ar-
rangements. Once I finally hooked up with Lonnie and
J.D. they were still busy trying to get the corpse looking
presentable. Figured I owed it to Turp to help. If I live
to be one hundred that will surely be about the hardest
thing I have to do.

We had to work on him in a side room at the back
of the church. It was a little Holiness church back off the
main road and the only water we could get to wash him
was from a well somebody had dug years ago on the other side of the graveyard that curled around the church
like a collar. The water had a touch of sulfur smell and
a reddish tint to it, which I'd been told meant that the
water was seeping through iron ore. If I'd been dying of
thirst I'd have had a hard time making myself drink it,
but that's what we used to wash the corpse of Turp Lawson.

Simply looking at any dead person made my brain
spin. Having it be somebody I knew was ten times worse.
Since I'd gone to bed with the dead man's wife it was almost more than I could stand. I carried water and tried
not to think of the bag of punctured skin and broken
bones as Turp. Long as I was outside toting a bucket of
water or looking at the names on the gravestones that
made it better, but once I got back inside that church
house it was pure misery.

All the time we were cleaning up the corpse I kept worrying about how we hadn't been able to get the Sheriff or somebody official like that to view the body. Didn't seem right to bury a man without a doctor or sheriff or judge or somebody with law connections viewed the corpse. I could picture all of us down at the state penitentiary in Eddyville for concealing a death, or some such violation. Laws can be tricky if you're not a lawyer. Plus, even though I knew Turp's death was an accident, plain and simple, deep down in my heart I still felt a twinge of guilt. Worst part was getting my suit on the boy. Turp had begun to swell and in the end we had to cut a slit up the back of the jacket and ease him into it. Holding one arm of that corpse almost made me pass out. By the time we had him ready I was trembling all over and sweating like a fat man eating fresh fried chicken.

Along toward evening people started showing up. Some of them I knew, at least to speak to. Others I'd never seen in my life. Figured they were crawling out from under rocks and walking down from the head of hollers just to see a dead man. A dead man, especially when he dies the way Turp did, is a big deal in Buhlan County.

Dusk had settled in solid when Mr. Whitman showed back up. He had Freeman Maggard with him. Freeman had been a magistrate and a constable for years and was currently the county coroner, and it eased my mind to have him view the body. Doyle Logan came in with them. When he wasn't working in timber, Doyle barbered and he'd brought his straight razor and had a go at shaving Turp's face. Shaving a dead man would have sent me over the edge.

Freeman had some official looking paper with him, and he and Mr. Whitman stood around the casket for some time, looking and pointing and talking low amongst themselves. Oh, they weren't trying to keep secrets, only talking low out of respect for the dead. I could have gone up there and listened to what they were saying, but I stood at the back of the little sanctuary and wondered how Marta was going to act when she laid eyes on me again. She had gone so crazy so quick I couldn't tell for sure if she was just over emotional or if she suspected me of killing Turp. When Freeman got to bending over and sorta examining the corpse I strolled outside.

Lonnie and a couple of the Hoskins boys was leaning against Lonnie's car and I wandered over and bummed a smoke. We were just starting to talk about who might run for Judge at the next election when headlights swept across the tombstones. Seconds later, two cars pulled into the parking lot and several women got out.

The light had gone chancy, but I could pick out Marta by her bright hair and the way she rolled her hips when she walked. Marta was with old Eliza Caney, who everybody called Granny, and some women I couldn't see plain enough to name. Probably was purely my imagination, but it looked like Marta glanced my way and smiled.

After we finished smoking and talking politics, the Hoskins boys allowed how they'd better be getting home and after a bit they meandered off into the dark. Part of me sure wished I was going with them.

Only I knew, after what I'd done, I had to stay. Staying wouldn't make things right, of course, and it sure wouldn't bring Turp back. But I figured maybe it would stand as a small atonement.

Lonnie and I went in and sat on the back bench. We didn't say much. Mainly just sat there listening to the women talk for a while, then cry for a while, then talk some more. Marta didn't say more than three words, just sat on the front row looking sad. Once, she went up and looked at the corpse for a time and I hoped we'd done a good enough job. On her way back to the pew she glanced at me and this time for sure she smiled.

Sitting there, a strange sort of wish came over me. What I wished for was a preacher to come in and talk to us a bit about how good God was and how He knew everything and how everything happened according to His purposes. Having Turp Lawson fall off a cliff and die didn't make any sense to me, but then I wasn't God.

Anyway, I figured hearing that preacher talk would ease some of the guilt that was eating away at my guts. Sure, I hadn't pushed Turp off that cliff, but I'd coupled with his wife, and, to tell the truth, I still wanted her. Hated myself for that, but it was the truth. No way could I lie in a church. Not even to myself. Somehow, what I'd done and what I still wanted to do made me feel like I'd played some part in what happened. My poor mind was so mixed up it reminded me of a nest of copperheads crawling all over each other. Way I was thinking, hearing a preacher might help me sort things out, at least a little.

But no preacher showed, and for sure nobody got up and preached a sermon. After a while J.D. did amble in and he gave me and Lonnie each a Baby Ruth candy bar. Eating in church wasn't a Christian way to act, but we ate them real quiet, out of respect. So maybe God didn't mind so much. J.D. also had a half-pint in his coat pocket and, when we were sure nobody was looking, we ducked down behind the pew and had a snort.

Somebody had built a fire in an old wood-burner at the back of the church and once they shut the door the little room warmed up in a hurry. Wasn't a big church. You might have stuffed fifty people in if you had to. My plan had been to stay awake; sit up with the dead, you might say. But, all in all, it had been a long, hard day and I kept getting sleepier. Lonnie and J.D. were whispering about the best way to skin a squirrel when I eased over against the corner of the pew and stretched my legs out under the pew in front of me. Sure was warm in that little church. My eyes felt full of sand.

11

WHEN I WOKE UP it was morning. At the far end of my pew Lonnie was snoring. We were the only two people in the little church. Except, that is, for Turp Lawson lying dead in his pine casket at the front. I wondered where everybody had gone and eased up off the pew and walked over to the little window in back. I was stiff all over like somebody had beat me with a broom handle while I slept.

It wasn't a stained glass window, although I wish it had been. Stained glass windows are one of the prettiest things man has ever made. If I didn't have to work, I could sit for hours gazing at the colors and patterns they create when sunlight passes through them. It's like they take something that is already pretty and make it purely beautiful. No one could rightly claim that I'm a religious man, but stained glass windows seem holy to me.

You could tell by the quality of the light that it hadn't been daylight long. First light of morning is like no other. Angling my head, I looked up. Clouds still rimmed the eastern horizon, but you could see clearing off to the west. Day promised to be clear by noon. I judged we'd carry Turp to his final rest in the sunshine. Then, I wondered what sort of day it would be when they shoveled dirt in my face.

I turned away from the window and looked down the aisle. In the first slants of daylight I could see dust motes dancing. My mother had said when the dust motes danced they were happy and that was a good omen. I wondered who they were an omen for. Then I remembered my mother had believed black cats were bad luck if they crossed in front of you and that a buckeye in your pocket warded off quinsy. Not to mention the way she got so excited Christmas Eve you'd swear she believed in Santa Claus.

Well, I sure as hell didn't believe in Santa Claus or the Easter Bunny and I'd begun to doubt the Lone Ranger. Life just seemed like hard knocks to me, and old Turp had given himself such a knock that he'd gone clean out of this world. I wondered if there really was another one after this one, or if this was the only chance we got. Thinking about stuff like that always made my brain hurt and I already felt like I was an old horse that had been rode hard and put up wet. Sleeping on that pew had made my back ache and my legs felt as stiff as fence rails.

Quiet filled that church until I caught myself holding my breath so as not to disturb it. Lonnie groaned once and then I guess he must have shifted on the pew because I didn't hear him snoring anymore. I stood at the back of the church, just looking around and trying to understand what was going on. After a bit, it occurred to me that other folks would be showing up soon and if I wanted a few minutes alone with Turp I'd better be moving.

Going down that aisle was a hard walk, a walk I sure didn't want to take. Yet it was one I felt I had to take if I was ever going to be able to stomach myself. I'll admit I was sweating by the time I got to the casket. Felt like guilt was dripping off me.

Turp's face was bruised up some, no denying that.

And no disputing he was dead. Also no use denying that it felt strange standing there looking down on a dead man wearing your only suit coat and knowing you'd gone to bed with his wife, and maybe would again. All of those thoughts made me feel sick to my stomach and it was all I could do to make myself stand there and look at him. Thank God, his eyes were closed. If they'd been open I swear it would have liked to have killed me.

My intention had been to walk up there and tell him I was sorry that he was dead, and I was sorry that I had slept with his wife, and I was sorry that I hadn't done more to help him that night. Don't know what I could have done, but about anything would have beat letting him go out and walk off the edge of a cliff. I was even sorry I hadn't been nicer to him when we worked together. Wouldn't have hurt me at all to smile at him now and then or stop and chat about the weather or how hard we was working. But I reckon all that regret was just the way life happens most of the time. Things and people we think are so important at the time eventually fade away. Like they say, we all have to go sometime. Only it seemed powerful early for Turp to pass. Seemed like he hadn't gotten a fair shake at all.

Well, I thought looking down on that battered face, I screwed your wife, buddy, and now you're wearing my suit and then after awhile I'm going to help carry you out of this church and bury you and somehow that all makes a crazy sort of sense.

All that was nothing but dime store philosophy, but sometimes even the most common man will say something profound. Still, it sure seemed to me we'd both paid too high a price.

I'd come intending to say a lot, hoping it would

purge my heart of grief and guilt. Only when I got up to the casket and looked at the skin and bones that had been a man, why I couldn't say nothing except to whisper real low, "I'm sorry." Maybe God or His angels heard me, but nobody else did, unless the dead can hear. And who am I to say?

Don't rightly know how long I stood there trying to make sense of death before its time and life that grew so complicated it made your brain crack. But in the end I didn't figure out even one damn thing. So I turned and went down the aisle and out into the promising sun. It was bright and warming up the morning and I was glad to be out in the living world and away from the church of the dead.

I fired up a smoke and strolled across the parking lot and turned south and walked about a mile to Junior Embry's store where I bought a can of Vienna sausages and a bottle of Nehi orange soda. I ate the Viennas and drank my Nehi sitting on a bench they called the liar's bench, trying to calm my mind by watching the traffic roll by. When I'd finished, I carried the empty bottle back inside, said a few words to Junior, then turned and started walking back toward the church. The sun had already climbed until it was almost overhead and the funeral was scheduled for high noon.

Snapshot

12

THE PREACHER WAS late. I'd never heard of the man, but did overhear Perry West telling Mr. Whitman that the preacher wasn't from around here. Some man I didn't know said the preacher had to come clear from Washoe Branch up in Knott County, but later I heard one of the women say that the preacher had only gotten out of the psycho ward at Central State a couple of weeks ago. She was one of those old women who come to funerals whether they knew the person or not.

Everybody just sat around whispering low and looking at each other out of the corners of their eyes. Then Mr. Whitman stood up and said it seemed to him that there ought to be some music and would some of the ladies mind to rise up and sing a gospel song or two, some hymns appropriate for a funeral. Granny Caney and a couple of other women stood up. They sang "The Old Rugged Cross" and "Crossing Over Jordan." Then they sang "Jesus Loves Me" and sat down. To tell the truth, they weren't much as singers.

After the singing, old Withrow Cordell stood up and read a couple of Psalms. Then we all sat around without anybody talking much. Once in a while I'd look up at the widow and at least twice when I did she was looking back at me. The second time she winked. After that, I shut my eyes and pretended I was asleep.

Guess I did doze off because Mr. Whitman's voice

jerked me awake. He was walking down the aisle, telling Perry West that he was going to get in his truck and try to find a certain preacher name of Brother Jesse. When they'd passed, I got up and followed them outside.

The day had turned off warmer than I'd figured. The sun was out most of the time and the wind had drifted up in the tops of the tallest oaks and maples. A rock wall ran along one side of the church yard and I walked over and sat down on it. Mr. Whitman and Perry West were already rolling down the asphalt. I tugged a cigarette out of my pocket and lit up, all the time wishing I had a half-pint in my hip pocket. Or at least a cold beer. Funerals gave me the willies.

I'd smoked about half my cigarette when the church doors opened and a few people came strolling out, blinking against the light. Marta was one of them. She was talking to Granny Caney, who was just a little old wizened up bird of a woman, and I could see Marta looking over the top of Granny's bonnet at me. Before I'd finished my cigarette a shadow fell across the toes of my boots. I looked up into the face of Turp Lawson's widow.

"Hey, Eddie," she said.

"Hello, Marta."

"What you doing?"

"Nothing much, just smoking a cig and waiting on the preacher to show."

She sat down beside me. She was wearing perfume. Today, Marta smelled like honeysuckle in bloom.

"Where you reckon that preacher's at?"

"Don't have a clue." I looked over at her. "You know the man?"

"Never seen him. Only thing I know is that he's Turp's cousin and a preacher. Turp said some people think Brother Jesse ain't quite in his right mind, at least not all the time, but I know Turp took pride in his cousin being a preacher. Talked about him a lot, Turp did."

Her voice broke a little when she said Turp's name and I stared at the ground. "You doing okay, Marta?"

"I'm doing fine," she said, "only missing you, Eddie. Thought you might come over last night and keep me company some." She patted my arm. Even for a woman she had small hands. "Maybe you could come over to-night?"

I gouged at the dirt with the toe of my boot. "That wouldn't be such a good idea, Marta. Turp has only just passed. Hell, he isn't even in the ground yet. People would talk."

"I don't care. It's lonely there at night without a man. I hear things moving and those noises scare me. Always have been the sort of girl that needs a man around to make her feel safe."

"Why don't you go and stay with your folks a few days? Just till your mind settles down."

"Oh, I couldn't do that. My dad is so strict. He wouldn't let me play cards or dance or nothing. Besides, he never liked Turp and I can hear him now mouthing about how I married a man so stupid that he took off all his clothes and went wandering around in the dark until he fell off a cliff. Oh no, Eddie, I couldn't stand that. I'm not sixteen no more. I'm a grown woman and I'm not going to be treated like no child." She put one hand on my knee and squeezed. "I've got urges, Eddie, grown woman urges. I'm not a child."

"I know you're not," I said, and gently pulled her hand off my knee, "but you've got to be careful 'bout what you do. You don't want everybody knowing your business."

"And why not? What do I care what they think? I'm my own woman and I'll live the way I want. Turp had some insurance. Enough to bury him and more beside. Only don't you tell anyone, you hear. Everybody thinks I'm just a poor young widow and they are ever so nice to me. Seems like a good idea to keep it that way, at least for now." Her hair brushed against one side of my face and tickled my ear. "That'll be our little secret, Eddie. We'll have lots of little secrets, you and me."

All of sudden, too quick for me to do anything, she lowered her head and kissed me flush on the mouth. Her lips were soft and her breath smelled like peppermint candies.

"Now give me a drag offen that cigarette, Eddie Burke. Been dying for a smoke all day."

I should have said something, protested what she had just done, but I didn't. Only handed her my cigarette and then snuck a quick glance around. Granny Carney must have gone to the outhouse and the only other person I could see was the youngest Lindsay boy and he was only a retard, one of those Mongoloid idiots.

Marta took a deep drag and blew smoke out her nose. Not many women around here smoked. I'd never seen any woman as young as Marta smoke. She took another drag and turned her head toward me and blew smoke in my face. Then she brushed her lips across mine and whirled and walked back toward the church. Halfway there, she dropped the cigarette butt on the ground. I watched her walk into the church. Her hips swayed and I was filled with lust. To lust after the widow of a man who had just died had to be a very wicked sin, but there wasn't one thing I could do about what I thought.

When she was inside, I pushed myself off the wall and walked over to where the youngest Lindsay boy stood. When he heard my footsteps, he turned and gave me his fool's grin. Real pity about that boy. His daddy was a school teacher and his mother gave piano lessons and read to the housebound.

13

TIME NEVER WAITS, not even for the dead. The day had grown old by the time Mr. Whitman got back with the preacher. Everyone had grown restless, except for old man Towe who'd been asleep for an hour. Couple of folks had even gone home, which wasn't bad because that little church couldn't hold many. Whole place was about the size of the banker's garage in town.

Brother Jesse and Mr. Whitman and Perry West walked into the church together, but Perry didn't go up front with the other two. He sat down on the other end of the pew I was resting on and I heard him whisper to one of the men between us that they'd drove clear down to the junction before they finally found the preacher kneeling in prayer alongside the highway. Then, they'd had to wait almost half an hour for him to finish.

Brother Jesse wasn't much to look at. Sure wasn't a big man. Might have been five feet six inches tall and couldn't have weighed more than one hundred and forty. He had longish brown hair like he was trying to look like Jesus you see in the paintings, or else had been praying so hard that he'd forgot to go to the barber.

His voice was pitched higher than normal for a man and squeaked when he got excited. Plus, he tended to spit some when he felt the power, which was another good reason for sitting on the back row.

Once he got rolling though, he could sure preach.

Fastest talking preacher I'd ever heard. Not that he preached what you'd call a funeral service. What he did was more like give a condensed version of the Bible. Started out with the Garden of Eden and went straight through Cain and Able and Moses and Daniel and lots of prophets whose names I get mixed up on and King David and Bathsheba. That one bothered me, I mean the part about lusting after another man's wife, especially with Marta sitting up on the front row and glancing back every so often. Brother Jesse made me remember when I'd read out of the Good Book to Asa, which made me seem like a messenger who fallen away.

So I quit listening. Oh, I'd hear a few words now and then—he said an awful lot about John the Baptist—but mostly I just thought about normal stuff, like had I remembered to give Trips fresh water, and what was I going to eat for supper, and how I'd have to go back to work on Monday, and how Turp was lying up there at the front in his pine box and my suit coat and how I'd messed around with his wife like King David had with Bathsheba. All that thinking made my head hurt, so I closed my eyes and let the words of Brother Jesse flow over me like a baptism of words.

Guess I slept a little, too, because I woke myself up snoring. I looked around to see if anybody had noticed and right off I could see the light had changed and the afternoon wouldn't last much longer.

Brother Jesse was still preaching and I think he'd have gone on till midnight, or till he passed out from hunger, whichever came first, only Mr. Whitman stood up when Brother Jesse paused for breath and said that it was against the law to bury a man after dark and we had better be moving.

Don't know anything about that law, but he was right about getting a move on. Perry West had told the widow that she could bury Turp in an old cemetery that belonged to his mother's folks, because they'd died out and wouldn't need any more plots. Problem was, that cemetery was clear at the top of Ross Mountain, which was dead on the county line, and nothing but bad roads, most of them gravel, to get there.

Brother Jesse gave him a look, but Mr. Whitman wasn't a man to be admonished by a look and one way or another the service got wrapped up. What finally did it was when Mr. Whitman asked the women to sing "Nearer My God to Thee" and even a preacher like Brother Jesse had to give way to a grand old hymn like that. That's the one the ship's band played when the Titanic was going down.

J.D. and Lonnie and I and three other fellows who worked for Mr. Whitman got up and went down the aisle and picked up the casket, which wasn't all that heavy, and carried it outside to Mr. Whitman's truck. His vehicle had good clearance and four-wheel drive, which Perry said we needed on account of the last stretch of gravel getting to the gravesite had been washed out by the summer rains.

Thought sure we was ready to go then. Even had the casket screwed down tight and up in the bed of the pickup when Marta started crying and carrying on like someone gone plain crazy. She was so wild nobody could figure out what was the matter, not even Granny Caney, and I went around on the other side of the truck in case it was me she was upset about.

Finally, Granny got her calmed down enough to find out what the problem was. Turned out that Marta was all upset because she didn't have a picture of Turp and she wanted one to frame and put on her mantle to remember him by.

I thought to myself what are you worried about a damn snapshot for when only this afternoon you was sitting on the rock fence putting your hand on my knee and talking about your womanly needs. But women they do think different than men; plus I was sure on the wrong side of this deal all the way round. So I just lit up a cigarette and smoked and looked at the sun going lower every minute while Mr. Whitman and Brother Jessie sorted it out. Wasn't any business of mine, even if I had made love to the dead man's wife and maybe not done enough to keep him from killing his crazy self. Just cause he was wearing my clothes didn't really signify.

In the end, the retarded Lindsay boy saved the day. Turns out his dad had bought him an old Kodak camera for a present one time and he said if somebody would give him a ride home why he'd fetch it and Mrs. Lawson could use it, sure, and no charge. Like I said, it was a pure shame about that boy's affliction. Easy to tell he came from a good home.

So Lonnie gave him a ride and the boy got the camera while we was getting the casket back down and standing it up against the bed of the pickup. Some of the mourners mumbled that it was a sin to open a casket, but Mr. Whitman and Perry West and the oldest Grimes boy done it anyway while the women sang a song I'd never heard before and Brother Jesse was a carrying on about turning wine into water and the dark days of the locust. All the while Marta was bawling and it was sure enough an awful time. Doubt if that Tower of Babel Brother Jesse had preached against earlier could have been much worse. Finally, they got back with the camera and Mr. Whitman took three pictures of Marta standing beside Turp in the casket and in the last one she was smiling.

Reckon those snapshots satisfied her, because she didn't carry on too bad when we closed the casket back up and nailed the lid down and hoisted the corpse back in the bed. Only she had to thank us all and hugged my neck and kissed me on the jaw which embarrassed the fire out of me. Believe me, I hightailed it around to the other side of Mr. Whitman's truck after that and hauled myself over the side of the bed. Figured it would be cold riding back there, so I snuggled down against the casket and tried not to think about Turp lying in his pine box, deader than a hammer and wearing my suit coat.

Mr. Whitman had to take it slow on account of the roads and the wind was down and we talked about deer hunting and when it would snow and smoked a little and every one wished somebody had brought along a bottle. Whiskey is sure the perfect remedy for a funeral.

One way or another we made that journey, and we dug old Turp's grave under a big old beech tree on the top of Ross Mountain and lowered him into the earth just as the sun was going down behind the far hills. Then we stood there for a few minutes while Mr. Whitman said a prayer that moved a man some. Afterwards, I stood a minute longer, praying silently for Turp and for Marta and finally for myself.

Also, I prayed some for forgiveness. Forgiveness for what I done, and for what I was sore afraid I was going to do again.

14

I CAME OUT of the dream with my mouth wide open and tears running down my face. One dripped onto my exposed tongue and I could taste the warm saltiness.

For a minute I was afraid I'd been talking in my sleep again, but Marta was still sleeping; I could hear her snoring. It wasn't an unpleasant sound, but I wouldn't call it gentle or ladylike, the way some writers describe the sleep sounds a woman makes. It was more like the faint rumblings a train makes when you hear one from a great distance off. Lately, part of me had been wishing I was riding on a train, no matter which direction it was rolling.

I eased the covers off and swung my legs out and walked soft to the window. On the eastern horizon the sky was trying to change. Morning's faint blue promise shimmered out there, but in the side yard darkness still held. A pale drift of moonlight covered the ground, silvering the roses Marta set such store by and causing the narrow stand of pine to throw crooked shadows at their feet. I pressed my face against the glass and stared out into what was left of another night.

The dream wasn't a new one. I'd had it, in one version or another, for weeks now. In fact, I had it regular ever since I'd moved in. It was dream that came at some point every night, but never quite finished. Some nights passages of it were different, but it always came around to seeing myself lying on my back in the middle of huge pile of rocks, every bone in my body broken and blood pouring out me like water. Only in the dream I can't feel any pain and I can't move. All I can do is lie there staring up at the sky, knowing I'm dying, thinking about all the things I wanted to do in my life and knowing for sure I wouldn't get them done now.

I tell you for certain that weeks of that are enough to break what's left of a man's mind and sorta get him hankering to die for real. Only I never quite die, not in the dreams and not when daylight comes. Only every morning I feel like I'm so knotted up inside that I can't move or think straight.

Nighttime is the time for thinking alright, even if the thoughts prick at your mind like a porcupine has somehow crawled up in there. Sleep is fitful these days. Doubt I get more than an hour or two at a time now. Makes a man feel sluggish and half stupid the next day, like his mind ain't quite right.

If I was my old self, the way I was before I got messed up with Turp Lawson, I'd be alright. Least ways I'd know my own mind and be able to take some sort of action, even it turned out wrong. But now that I'm living with Marta it seems like I can't hardly decide anything anymore. Why, there are days when I have trouble picking out which shirt to wear.

Funny thing is that's it not really Marta that's messing up my mind so. Oh, she's still one fine looking woman and real good in bed. I like lots about her. No, it's not Marta. Tell the truth, it's Turp, or maybe his spirit, if there can be such a thing.

He's dead alright. I know that. Hell, I helped bury him, and him wearing my clothes. And down deep I know there's no such thing as ghosts. Only sometimes I see him so plain in my mind that he might as well be real.

The bedsprings squeaked then and I twisted around and looked across the room. Marta had turned over on her side and now her face was full in the moonfall and she looked sorta the way I've always pictured an angel looking and sorta like a little girl pretending grownup. Her eyes were still closed, but I still had the sense that she was seeing me somehow, so I spun on my heel and tiptoed out of the bedroom.

For a couple of weeks now I'd kept a bottle in the top cupboard, behind a row of Mason jars full of green beans Marta had canned. When the night visions got too heavy for me to bear I'd slip out and have me a shot, or two. If Marta knew about the bottle she was keeping it to herself.

Trips was lying in front of the stove, and he lifted his head and opened one eye long enough to make sure who I was. I bent and rubbed him right between the eyes and he lowered his head and shut his eyes.

Moving as quietly as I could, I took down one of the Mason jars and eased the bottle out. Then I got a glass down out of the cupboard and carried them both over to the rocking chair in the parlor.

It would have been nice to have somebody to share a drink with me and talk to some, say J. D. or Lonnie. But it was only me and Trips and he'd already gone back to sleep, snoring the way only a dog can. So I sat the whiskey and the empty glass down on Marta's coffee table, the one her mama gave her, the one where Marta kept the picture of her and Turp, with him in his coffin, and I poured myself a stiff one.

Chris Helvey

119

The color of that whiskey put me in mind of old Asa and I wondered how he was doing. I reckoned he sure enough must live a lonesome life, but it seemed to me that there was more than one kind of lonesome. I wondered if his old eyes were too far gone now to read the Bible and if his son still came regular to see him and if he would be all alone when he died.

Turp had surely been all alone when he died. But then, in a certain way, I figured when the end came every man was ultimately alone. Maybe God was there. Maybe not.

For a bit I just sat there and rocked, listening to Trips snoring and the house creak and groan the way a house does at night when it thinks all the people are asleep. There was sharp chill to the air at night now and I gave some thought to getting up and getting me a sweater, but in the end I didn't. Instead I lifted my glass and nodded at Turp in his coffin and took me a hefty sip.

For I can't say how long, I only sat there, rocking back and forth like some old granny woman, staring that picture of Turp in its cheap brassy frame Marta had bought at the Dollar Store, thinking about Marta and what I wanted to do, or ought to do, and how I could quit dreaming that dream.

But like the other nights, I never came up with a satisfying answer. I simply rocked and stared at the Polaroid of old Turp in his coffin and wondered how I might have somehow made it all turn out different and considered how there were a lot of different ways of dying and how not all coffins were the same.

Photo: Clay Gibson

Chris Helvey's poems and short stories have been published in numerous reviews and journals. He is also the author of *On The Boulevard, Purple Adobe, Whose Name I Did Not Know,* and *Claw Hammer.* He currently serves as editor and publisher of *Trajectory Journal* and as an editor for *Best New Writing.* He lives and writes with his wife Gina in Frankfort, Kentucky.